PUMPKIN SPICE
and
HAUNTED NIGHTS

A Collection of Fall Stories
from the
Chesapeake Bay Writers

BLUE FORTUNE ENTERPRISES LLC

PUMPKIN SPICE AND HAUNTED NIGHTS
Copyright © Narielle Living 2025.

All rights reserved. Printed in the United States of America. No part of this book may be used or reproduced in any manner whatsoever without written permission except in the case of brief quotations embodied in critical articles or reviews.

This book contains works of fiction. Names, characters, businesses, organizations, places, events and incidents either are the product of the author's imagination or are used fictitiously. Any resemblance to actual persons, living or dead, events, or locales is entirely coincidental.

For information contact :
Blue Fortune Enterprises, LLC
Lavender Press
P.O. Box 554
Yorktown, VA 23690
http://blue-fortune.com

ISBN: 978-1-961548-34-3

First Edition: September 2025

Dedication

*This collection is dedicated to the storytellers among us, the
people who share their vision and inner landscapes, the
people who create worlds and sustain us with their stories.
Our lives would be much darker without you.*

Table of Contents

Dear Reader,

You have probably heard from writers how lonely the art of writing can be. Writing fiction means creating worlds and inventing new people and sometimes researching history, but it is all done from the confines of our home office or desk or kitchen table or coffee shop. We have little to no contact with office workers and often our only interaction is between ourselves and our search engines.

This is the reason that the Chesapeake Bay Writers (CBW) group is a vital part of the writing community here in the Tidewater area of Virginia. We have a social media presence, we have meetings, and we can turn to each other for help when needed.

The mission of CBW is to support writers in all stages of their writing journey, from the nuts and bolts of putting together a manuscript, to editing, to publication, and everything in between. It can be daunting to travel from page one to publication, but writers' groups are always ready to help new and seasoned writers.

If you are a writer and looking for a home, I suggest you reach out to your local writers' group. If you cannot find one, email me at narielle@blue-fortune.com. I would be happy to help.

This second collection of stories from the fabulous CBW writers is all Halloween themed: from monsters to ghosts to demon justice, we hope these stories entertain and inspire you.

Thank you,

Narielle Living
Editor

Feeding Time

Carl J. Shirley

October 31, 2018
York County, Virginia

"Oh look, it's Iron Man!" The woman dropped two pieces of candy into the hollow plastic Jack-o'-lantern and waited for the boy's "thank you," barely audible through the gold and red plastic mask, before moving on to the next child. "And Captain America." She quickly saluted the boy before placing his candy into the red, white, and blue bag. "The Hulk." The next child wore a bulging green mask and two oversized, matching plastic fists haphazardly duct-taped to a pillowcase. The last of the four children was a girl dressed in a shiny black jumpsuit and a bright orange wig. "And who are you, dear?" the woman asked.

"Black Widow," the girl whined and stomped her foot, but remembered to say thank you before following the others off the porch.

"Has anyone even seen those movies?" she asked as they reached the sidewalk.

"No," Iron Man said. "They made a trillion dollars without anybody seeing them." He pushed the mask up, revealing his face, an exact, if smaller, replica of the face of the actor Robert Downey, Jr. "What did everyone get?" he asked, peering into his bag. "I got a couple of peanut butter cups."

"A chocolate bar," Captain America reported.

"Same here." Black Widow sighed.

"I got a rock." The Hulk was gone, replaced by a sheet covered from top to bottom with empty black eyeholes.

"You know when that stopped being funny?" Robert asked. "1974."

"It's a classic." The sheet evaporated into the warm October night. The child beneath, to all appearances a nine-year-old boy with a blond crew cut, had traded his Hulk mask and hands for an eye patch and a plastic sword.

"Don't change on the street," Captain America said.

"And try to remember this year's theme," Robert added.

"I'm tired of this year's theme," Black Widow said. "Nobody recognizes me." The shiny black material of her

S.H.I.E.L.D. jumpsuit melted and swirled into brown buckskin as the unkempt red-orange wig straightened into long black hair. An ornate headband with an eagle feather popped into place around her head to complete the look.

"That's a culture, not a costume," Captain America noted.

"I'm not a culture; I'm a historical person named Pocahontas." Her skin darkened as she spoke.

"How does that match the pirate?" Robert asked.

"Most of the European people Pocahontas met were pirates," she explained.

Captain America's costume morphed into the blue and gold uniform of an early nineteenth-century U.S. naval officer, his mask transforming into a matching blue bicorn hat that migrated to the top of his head.

"We're supposed to be *The Avengers,* people," Robert started. "Now, who the hell are you supposed to be?" he asked the sea captain.

"The original Captain America, John Paul Jones."

"Clever." Robert pulled his mask back down and started toward the next house. "You can explain that to people."

"So, we're giving this house a pass?" Pocahontas asked. "I smell guilt."

"You're just mad that she didn't know who you were," Robert replied.

"I smell embezzlement," the pirate added.

"So, she took a couple of hundred dollars from the church mission fund," Robert said. "And she feels guilty as hell, but let's face it, her sin has no flavor. You get to feed one night a year. Let's skip the tofu burger and find a bloody rare steak."

A poorly carved jack-o'-lantern lit the porch of the sixth house down, casting orange light from its lopsided eyes and jagged grin. Robert adjusted his Iron Man mask and rang the doorbell. A man dressed in loose jeans, a black, long-sleeved T-shirt, and a green rubber Frankenstein mask appeared with a bowl of candy. "Tricks or treats," the four children shouted.

"Frankenstein have treats," the man mimicked the monster with his broken, halting speech. "Me have treat for Iron Man." He dropped some candy into the container. "For pirate. For sea captain."

"John Paul Jones," the former Captain America explained.

"And one for Sacajawea." The Indian princess watched as he dropped the candy into her bag.

"Thank you," she said. The others echoed her as they sped off the porch.

"Now, that's the one," John Paul Jones said as they reached the street.

"I think so," Pocahontas said.

"Most definitely," Robert agreed.

"So, who goes back?" the pirate asked.

"Why, the princess, of course," Robert stated, leading them past a half dozen cars parked on the street and behind a tall hedge.

"Why her?" John Paul Jones asked.

"This one likes the girlies," Robert said. "Your energy is too masculine."

"I'm a 12,000-year-old shape-shifting demon," Jones noted. "My energy can be whatever I want it to be."

"Yeah, I don't think so," Robert said. "Remember when you tried to infiltrate that convent in Calais? How many centuries did you spend in a hudiča after that?"

"Hey, don't say the c-word." Jones shivered. "Go ahead then, princess. Bait the trap."

"Not like that," Robert said.

"Yeah," Pocahontas agreed. "Wrong victimology. Too cute. Too young."

"Victimology?" Jones sighed and turned to the pirate. "Ya know, I used to command the Legions of Dargolthalen. Once, I even laid siege to the Gates of Heaven. Now I'm in an episode of *Law and Order: SVU*."

"Calais," the pirate said. Jones shivered again.

"How old?" Pocahontas asked. "Fourteen? Fifteen?"

"Na," Robert answered. "Too far in the other direction. Thirteen, I think—everyone's lucky number."

Pocahontas took a deep breath and began her

transformation, growing taller as her clothes and features melted and transformed. She changed from a faux nine-year-old Native American princess to a thirteen-year-old goth girl, her skin a shade of pale just the living side of death, and her collar-length hair raven black. She wore black jeans and a short-sleeved black T-shirt with the word Poison on the front, partially covered by an olive drab jacket without buttons. Black lipstick, eyeliner, and a trio of eyebrow piercings over her left eye finished the look.

"Yeah, yeah," Robert said. "That's close, but lose the lipstick and two of the piercings and lighten up a little on the eyeliner."

"Goth but not too goth," the girl agreed as she adjusted her features.

"Right, you're not just alienated from civilized society; you're even alienated from uncivilized society."

"It's fine either way," Jones observed. "The predator will predate no matter how you decorate the prey."

"My art is wasted on you," Robert said to Jones before turning back to the girl. "But he's right. This will work fine."

"And don't forget our invitations," the pirate added.

"Never," the girl agreed as she walked from behind the hedge.

The jack-o'-lantern flickered as the flame inside sputtered and died, consuming whatever remained of wax and wick with its final burning. It was a quarter past the county's curfew for trick-or-treating when she climbed the creaky steps up to the porch, which stretched across the front of the old house. An atonal chime sounded as she rang the doorbell, followed by the clomping of the monster's shoes. "Tricksertreats," she mumbled after the monster opened the door, compressing the phrase into a single word. He reached into his candy bowl and pulled out a full-size Three Musketeers bar. "It's past the curfew," the monster noted as he dropped the candy into her bag.

"Yeah, I'm running late," she replied.

"A little old to be trick or treating, aren't you?"

"Just a year."

"Only a year?" The monster reached under the rubber mask and peeled it off. "You look older than that to me. Why are you bothering with this kid stuff?"

"Didn't have nothin' better to do," she said. Without his mask, the man was average, attractive even in an everyman sort of way, with short brown hair and hazel eyes. The girl recalled a phrase regarding the banality of evil.

"I'd have thought someone your age would be interested in something more adult."

"Like what?"

"You like beer?" he asked.

"Nobody likes beer," she sneered.

"So, something with more flavor. C'mon in and I'll see what I have." He casually went back into the house, the screen door clapping against the frame as the front door remained open. The casualness was part of the trap. He didn't really care whether she came into the house or not. She was free to leave. She would hesitate for effect, but the invitation had already been made.

Inside, the dark house smelled of vice and violence, of decades of the sinful and the sordid, accumulating in the walls and absorbed by the carpets. It was an evil house that had been a breeding ground for monsters for decades. And it all seemed somewhat under-maintained. Worn forest green carpet with a faded pattern. Wood paneling from the last century showing every bit of its age. A staircase was to the right, and a couch was positioned against the left wall. The girl stood there, just inside the still-open door, and waited.

The monster returned, carrying two short glasses, half-filled with a clear, brown liquid. "Here's something with a little more kick," he said as he handed her a glass. She looked at the drink, hesitating. "Why don't you take a seat?" He gestured toward the couch, and she walked over and sat down. The monster kept his distance. "To Halloween." He raised his glass and drank. The girl responded in kind.

The liquid was bitter and tasted like burnt wood. She could taste every molecule as they washed into her mouth, the atomic bonds dissolving as they crashed against her nature, the chains of hydrogen, carbon, and oxygen that made up the whiskey breaking apart alongside another more exotic compound. She could not identify that particular chain of molecules, but she knew what it was designed to do.

"So, you live around here?" the monster asked.

"No," she responded. "I don't need the neighbors reporting to my parents." She took another large swallow of the drink.

"So, your parents don't know where you are?"

"Snot cealy," she slurred.

"Finish your drink," he urged as he walked over to the door. She raised the drink to her lips but did not complete the action, as the glass fell out of her hand, and she fell back onto the couch. The monster closed and locked the door, switched off the porch light, and walked over to the girl. "You okay?" he asked, poking a finger into her shoulder. She did not respond.

He grabbed her by the ankles and pulled her off the couch. She crashed against the floor with a thud, still appearing unconscious. He dragged her over to a door in the staircase. He opened it, pulled the girl inside, and then dragged her down a set of ancient wooden stairs into the basement. He ran upstairs to close the basement door and then back down to his prize. He lifted her off the cold concrete floor and stripped off her jacket before placing her face up on a narrow bed, a bare spring mattress devoid of any padding. He stepped over to a workbench and grabbed a pair of scissors.

He paused for a moment in anticipation, hovering over her, trying to decide where to cut first. He lifted the front of her T-shirt, the razor-sharp jaws of the scissors starting to close when she spoke. "Don't do that." Her voice had dropped an octave, filling the room with a gravelly echo. "It really is my favorite T-shirt." He looked up and stared into her eyes, her pupils now glowing bright orange. He tried to pull away but could not move; the girl's hands had clamped around his arms. The monster's body became rigid as she levitated them three feet off the mattress and flipped him over, pressing him down into the bare wires, which snaked up and wrapped tightly around his extremities. "Look up there," she commanded, nodding toward the basement window. Iron Man, John Paul Jones, and the Pirate were looking in. "Invite them in."

"What?" the monster asked.

"Invite them in," she roared, the wires from the mattress tightening as they cut through his clothes and into his skin.

"Come in, come in," the monster said. Glass shattered as the boys poured through the window. "What are you?" the monster asked. "Vampires?"

"Don't be silly," the girl smiled. "There's no such thing as vampires." Her smile widened across her face, filling with row after row of needle-sharp teeth. She laughed again, her jaw unhinging as she bit into his shoulder.

About the Author

Carl J. Shirley was born and raised in Norfolk, Virginia. A graduate of the original Norfolk Catholic High School and later Old Dominion University, Carl works as the Planning Director for a nonprofit community action agency located in Newport News. In the more productive moments of his spare time, he writes fiction, mostly science fiction and other popular genre novels and short stories. He also enjoys history, astronomy, photography, hiking, biking, good movies, and better books.

A Corduroy Halloween Wedding

Patti Gaustad Procopi

Sequal to A Corduroy Christmas from the book
Christmas on the Bay

The embarrassing and sad ending to our 1973 Christmas continued to affect us all. My mother, while not a fan of Tony as a potential suitor of her daughter, Lexi, prided herself on her hospitality and southern graciousness. The fact that a guest in her home felt the need to storm out in the middle of the night filled with anger at the family was quite vexing.

Dad, while possibly glad Tony would not be joining the family as a permanent member, was appalled a guest of theirs almost burned the house down by shoving an offending corduroy suit into a fireplace and setting it on fire.

I didn't think Tony intended to burn down the house with us asleep in our beds. I just assumed he didn't know much about fireplaces and didn't know the flue was closed.

And Lexi. Sigh. What could I say about Lexi? While she tried to pretend it was for the best, I knew she still held me partly, if not completely, responsible for what transpired. "If only you hadn't let him buy that horrible, inappropriate, unattractive, cheap, vile suit," she said. She actually didn't say it but when she looked at me and her mouth turned down, I knew that was exactly what she was thinking.

We all hoped to never see or confront Tony again. Lexi had already transferred to the local college, so she was safe in Williamsburg. I also hoped that I could transfer and stay at home, rather than return to college in New York, where there was a good chance I'd run into Tony since he taught there.

However, my father informed me, since he'd already paid for my second semester, including room and board, I would have to go back and finish the year. Then I could transfer to another college for my second year.

Lexi, no doubt, thought it was just punishment for my crimes against her and humanity in general. I still did not understand how one ugly suit could have caused so much grief and turmoil.

At the end of Christmas break, I found myself in a

taxi from the airport on the way to college. I considered dyeing my hair and wearing thick, fake glasses so if Tony happened to catch a glimpse of me, he wouldn't recognize me. But how would I explain my altered appearance to the other students who knew me? I just took to wearing floppy hats when I walked around campus.

For the first couple of months, I luckily did not run into Tony. Since he taught in the art department and I was majoring in history and literature, we were not in each other's spheres. I stayed on my side of the campus, and I hoped he would stay on his.

Inevitably, unfortunately, it happened. I was hurrying to class one day and suddenly there he was. Only ten feet in front of me. We both stopped. And stared.

"You…" he stammered. "What are you doing here?"

"I go to school here, remember?" I said, trying to look cool and superior. How dare he question me as to why I was there. He didn't own the college. He was just a lowly art professor.

I tried to sweep past him with my head held high, but he grabbed my elbow as I passed.

"Izzie, wait, can we talk? I need to talk to you. I'm so sorry for how I behaved."

Well, that was a good opening. At least he seemed to be over blaming me and my entire family for the disastrous holiday.

"Do you have time to go for a coffee?" he asked, naked

pleading in his eyes. "I have been so miserable. So full of remorse…" he let that sentence dangle as he moved me toward a coffee shop, not even waiting for my answer.

The bell jingled as we entered, and Tony said he'd grab the coffee. "Cream and sugar, right? How about a pastry? I know you like apple Danish." I nodded and sat down and waited for him. I hoped this would be a quick apology and we could forgive each other and move on. I'd be happy not to have to slink around campus in a big hat.

He joined me at the table and set a hot coffee and Danish in front of me. Then we looked at each other. He didn't speak. I wasn't going to start. This was his dog and pony show. He said he wanted to apologize. I almost said, "Okay get on with it." But I bit my tongue.

Sighing deeply, he looked down at his coffee, hoping to find—courage? Enlightenment? Encouragement?

Finally, he looked up and opened his mouth. "I don't even know where to start. First, I want to apologize to you. I know the whole disaster wasn't your fault."

At last, someone was finally acknowledging that fact. I wanted to ask, "Can I record you?" I didn't have a tape recorder with me, but I could drag him to a phone and have him tell Lexi he didn't blame me.

I decided to be gracious. "I'm sorry too for how badly things went. I should have told you not to buy such an awful corduroy suit."

Tony threw back his head and laughed. "Oh my God.

It was ugly, wasn't it? How did I ever think I would fit in with Virginia society in that monstrosity? But in my defense, it was the only suit I'd purchased since my first communion when I was twelve. And my mother bought that one. And I remember the fabric was some kind of slick, black, shiny stuff. It was awful too, so I don't have a good track record with suits."

I smiled. He smiled. A great weight was lifted off me. I'd always liked Tony, and I was glad to put it behind us.

"But I want to apologize to your mother and father as well. Which I can hardly do in person," Tony said. "What do you suggest?"

Now, I was the wise counselor, healing the wounds. "Flowers are always good. Yes, flowers. And a note saying how much you enjoyed meeting them, thanking them for their hospitality and apologizing for your abrupt departure."

"Flowers…" Tony looked thoughtful. "That's a good idea. I'll order some tomorrow. And include a note."

"I believe it would really help." I smiled at Tony and took a sip of my coffee. It was great. Then I took a bite of the Danish.

I was chewing thoughtfully when Tony said, "And what about Lexi? How can I make it up to her?"

I almost spit the Danish out across the table. Oh, no. I told myself, I am not being dragged into their drama again.

"Oh, wow, look at the time. I'm late for class." I jumped

up and gathered my things, including my Danish. I earned it.

"Please… I need your help, Izzie. No one knows your sister like you do." Tony blushed, looking down. "I… still love her… I can't live without her…"

"Tony, I don't know what to tell you. She's moved on… dating other people… you know how it goes…"

He grabbed my hand and kissed it. "Please. You are my only ally, my only link to your sister. She listens to you. If you told her to give me a chance to apologize, she'd listen. Seriously, it's all I want to do. Apologize."

I raised my eyebrows. "Seriously? That's all?"

"It's a start… and one thing might lead to another."

"I've really got to go," I said and practically ran out of the café.

Now that Tony knew I was on campus, he could hunt me down. He popped up everywhere—after class, before class, in the dining hall, in the library. I thought I'd lose my mind.

The other students smiled at me. "Oh, my goodness, he's quite the catch and obviously smitten with you."

"I'm going to report you," I hissed angrily. "You can't be stalking me like this. If you want to talk to Lexi, call her. Leave me out of it. The last time I got involved, you two ended up blaming me for everything and you almost burned us alive when you set fire to your ugly suit."

He wore me down. Finally, I agreed to talk to Lexi and just tell her he wanted to apologize.

So, I called. We chatted about various things. Classes. The weather. Old friends and new. It was now or never. "Did I tell you I ran into Tony on campus?" I asked, trying to sound innocent. "He is so guilt ridden over his behavior."

"Oh yes. He sent the most beautiful flowers to Mother with a note begging her forgiveness." I wanted to say the Catholics are good with those acts of contrition, walking on their knees halfway across Europe and back.

Instead, I said, "Oh, how nice of him." Of course I didn't mention it had been my idea. "He wants to apologize to you as well." There, I said it. The words were out of my mouth and in the air.

There was silence on the other end of the line. I thought we'd become disconnected when finally, Lexi cleared her throat. "You know," she said, "I actually have felt really bad about the whole thing as well."

It was a good start.

"I mean, the suit was ugly. Oh my God." She laughed. "Seriously beyond ugly but I should have known he wouldn't know how to dress for a Williamsburg Christmas."

I bit my tongue, almost suggesting she could start the whole forgiveness process by apologizing to me, her sister, who'd done everything in her power to make Tony and Lexi's Christmas a wonderful experience. But, as usual, this wasn't about me.

"How fabulous you've come to that conclusion. Sooo… can he call you? Just to say he's sorry."

"I think it would be acceptable."

And so it began. The beginning of them deciding once again they were meant to spend the rest of their lives together. In wedded bliss. Seriously? I knew one thing. I would not be involved in picking out the wedding suit.

At the end of the semester, I arrived back home with all my worldly goods. I had already planned on going back to Virginia for the rest of my college career. I found being around Lexi and Tony to be emotionally exhausting and I didn't want to be where they were. And if they broke up again, I didn't want to be within a thousand miles of Tony hunting me down and begging me to help him win Lexi back. Not my problem.

I found Lexi in full-blown conspiracy mode. First, she talked to Mom and Dad and asked if it would be all right for Tony to come for another visit. A make-up visit, as it were. The stress of the holidays had proven too much for everyone, and things naturally spiraled out of control.

While our mother had been softened by the flowers and Tony's note of apology, I knew she was secretly relieved Lexi and Tony had broken up. However, before she could open her mouth and suggest letting sleeping dogs lie, our father, who usually left all social events in the capable hands of our mother, looked up from his newspaper and said, "That's a great idea. I also felt bad about how things went. We can show him some proper Southern and Colonial hospitality this time."

Mom appeared about to explode from the strain of keeping her emotions in check. Her face turned six shades of purple, and her mouth screwed up into a tight knot. She was finally able to calm down but before she could explain why it might not be a good idea, Lexi jumped up and hugged Dad and said, "Oh Daddy, thank you." Just to be on the safe side, she hugged and kissed Mom on the cheek as well before she rushed out of the room. "I'm going to call him and set a date."

The look my mother shot at my father could have killed an entire battalion but Dad was oblivious since he'd turned back to the newspaper. Before she turned it on me, I fled.

A date was set. This time Tony arrived by train. It was a lot less expensive than flying. Lexi took Dad's car and picked him up at the train station. The charming little Williamsburg train station. The train ride from New York took almost an entire day since the train stopped at every town on the way. I was not required to chauffeur this time since the station was only a twenty-minute ride to our house at First Landing Estates. This time the sun was still up, and the houses were not decorated with over-the-top Christmas décor following the annual theme. Tony was met with simple, gorgeous, manicured lawns and gardens.

Lexi planned a full schedule of events for Tony's two-week visit, including the beach and every museum from Norfolk to Richmond. As an artist, Tony was particularly interested in the art museums but was dragged along to historic sites and museums as well. I knew she was just trying to keep him away from Mom as much as possible.

Tony stayed down in the basement room again for this visit. It had been re-painted and refurbished after the smoke damage from the fire. No mention was made of that event.

Occasionally we'd have dinner together, including a return visit to the country club, one of the scenes of the initial Christmas debacle when Tony wore the awful corduroy suit for the first time to the horror of Lexi, confusion of my father, and shame of my mother. This dinner went a lot more smoothly.

I was hoping no one even remembered Tony from Christmas. He'd cut his hair and shaved his four-inch-long sideburns. He had a normal wardrobe of khakis and polos, and nothing made out of corduroy. On the other hand, it was summer, so hardly the season for corduroy. But is it ever the season for corduroy?

After two weeks, it was time for Tony to leave and head back home. We stood in the hallway, shaking hands and wishing him a safe trip. There was no hugging. Mom was still trying to control the various emotions playing across her face: fear, anxiety, but mostly relief he was almost gone and hopefully would stay gone.

Tony and Lexi continued to talk on the phone every weekend. One night at dinner she announced Tony had invited her up to meet his family. "Well, just his mom and uncle. He doesn't have a very large family."

I thought my mother would spit out the food in her mouth. She knew what it meant to be invited to meet someone's mother. This was swiftly spiraling out of her control.

And so, Lexi left to meet Mrs. G., the Italian mother. This time I drove her to the train station.

"Are you nervous?" I asked as I hauled her suitcase out of the trunk.

"No. I'm sure she's one of those sweet old ladies. Always cooking and hugging you."

She returned a week later. When our parents asked how the visit was, she gushed. "Wonderful. Such a devoted mother. And his uncle is also great."

But upstairs, she told me a different story. "It was awful. Just awful," Lexi said, throwing herself down on the bed and covering her head with a pillow. "The woman seriously never smiles. Well, at least not at me. She dresses in all black. Tony said she's worn black since his father passed away over twenty years ago."

"Ugh." I couldn't think of anything else to say. Maybe this would be the death knell of their future. Who wants a mother-in-law like that?

"And Uncle Vinnie was straight out of one of those gangster movies, like *The Godfather*. Both Tony's mother and uncle were straight out of central casting."

But it wasn't the death knell. The summer continued to be an emotional revolving door. Tony came down again and asked Dad for Lexi's hand. Of course, he asked with Lexi standing right next to him with a grin so wide and bright it could have lit up the entire town. So, what could Dad do? He said yes, and he and Tony shook hands and Lexi hugged Dad and then hugged Tony. Then they went to tell my mother the "happy news." She was obviously not happy but resigned.

"We want to get married this fall," Lexi said. "I love the colors and smells of autumn. Pumpkin spice. Apple cider."

Was she going to mention every aspect of fall?

"I'll have to call the club and get it booked. You know they book fast."

And they did. The only day available was Halloween. Mother was appalled. "No one gets married on Halloween," she announced. Firmly. She was no doubt relieved with the news. If she could put the wedding off to the next year, maybe the relationship would collapse one more time.

"Oh, I think it would be wonderful," Lexi gushed. "We can tell everyone to come in costume. Maybe I could dress up as the Bride of Frankenstein. And Tony could be…"

A gorilla in a corduroy suit, I thought but did not say.

Despite Lexi and Tony floating ideas that the guests should dress in corduroy to memorialize the infamous suit or dress in Halloween costumes, Mother was able to convince them to just have a normal wedding.

Lexi decided not to go back to school for the fall semester, either in Williamsburg or New York. "I have a wedding to plan. That takes precedence over everything," she announced. I wouldn't be surprised if she never returned to class. She was not what I would call a devoted student. Now, she'd be a faculty wife, which would be a big step up in the college social scene.

Luckily, since I was firmly ensconced in Virginia, I

was also available to help with all the wedding plans. Shopping for dresses, deciding on the menu and the decorations. Lexi wanted a full-out fall theme, though mother had nixed any nod to Halloween. Despite Lexi marrying Tony, Mother seemed quite thrilled planning a big wedding at the club. Before we knew it, October was almost over. The wedding of the year, as mother liked to describe it was almost upon us.

A few days before the wedding, a black limousine-type car with a trunk big enough to hold several bodies showed up. It was Uncle Vinnie, Momma G., and Tony. Tony jumped out full of grins and happiness as he helped his mother from the car and up to our house.

Lexi hadn't exaggerated when she described this dour, sour little woman. She looked at all of us as if we were dirt and stared at Mom and Dad's gorgeous home as if it was a hovel. Lexi told me Momma G. lived in a third-floor walk-up apartment that was hot, smelly, and tiny, so I don't know why she was acting so superior.

My mother, to give her credit, smiled and graciously welcomed Tony's mother to the house. Momma G. curled a lip and began muttering in Italian to Tony and Vinnie. At least I assumed it was Italian.

"Oh, I didn't realize your mother didn't speak English," my mother said with a bit of sarcasm.

Tony blushed furiously and glared at his mother. "Oh no. She speaks English."

But if she did, she wasn't going to share her gift with us.

Tony carried her suitcase up to one of the guest bedrooms. Uncle Vinnie was relegated to the apartment over the garage, which Lexi assured me was much nicer than their apartment back in New York. He grabbed his suitcase and followed my father without a word of thanks or greeting.

This was going to be a difficult week. In many respects, this was worse than an ugly suit. This was two mothers who already hated each other and didn't want their children to marry.

Momma G. was also apparently outraged the wedding ceremony would take place at a Protestant church. There would be no Catholic priest blessing this marriage. That led to more mutterings, which sounded suspiciously like curses and threats.

Mother busied herself with Lexi, the two of them going over all the last-minute details. I hung out with them. The day before the wedding, Momma G. took over Mother's kitchen and began furiously baking.

"It's an Italian thing," Tony explained, though he looked nervous and unhappy with his mother. "You must have wedding cookies. I'm sorry, I know she should have asked for permission to use the kitchen."

"That's fine," my mother said through a clenched jaw. "We're all family here."

If anyone got close to the kitchen they were greeted by furious Italian and threatened with a large wooden spoon shaken in their face.

As I was carrying a plate of cookies out to the dining room, I picked one up. I wanted to see what they tasted like. Before I could raise the cookie to my mouth, I was struck on the wrist with the wooden spoon and soundly yelled at. The cookie hit the ground and was snatched up by Momma G. Finally, she said something in English. "Cookies for wedding. Only for wedding."

I mumbled an apology and returned to carrying trays of cookies out to the dining room. After they cooled, they were packed up in huge plastic containers which Momma G. brought with her. No dead bodies in the trunk, just plastic. We were to take them to the club the morning of the wedding.

The wedding went off without a hitch. Lexi was a beautiful bride. Tony looked good in a tailored tux. His mother was a blot on the day, swathed in black with Uncle Vinnie in his mobster-style suit, leading her to their seats. The other guests tried not to stare. There was the constant muttering of Momma G. as she looked around our lovely church as if it was a den of iniquity. When the priest asked if anyone objected to the wedding, I saw her start to stand up, but Uncle Vinnie grabbed her and forcefully sat her down.

Our parents were, of course, gorgeous and gracious. The meal the club served was fabulous. Mother even made a lovely speech about Momma G.'s cookies, which turned out to be delicious.

We danced until dawn. Well, at least past midnight and then made our way back home. I collapsed in my bed, so happy it was over. Tony and Lexi were married. Now, she could move to New York, move into a tiny apartment, and live the Bohemian lifestyle, which I didn't think suited her. On the other hand, maybe Tony would take up my dad's offer to come work for him, and Lexi could live the country club life she was meant to live.

I woke to hear angry voices coming from downstairs. Not again! I jumped up, grabbed my robe, and ran down the steps. Tony, Lexi, and the two mothers were in the living room. The mothers seemed to be shouting at each other in two different languages. Momma G. held Tony by the arm and was yanking him away from Lexi, who was clinging to him desperately. Mother had Lexi by the arm as well, yanking her away from Tony.

Déjà vu all over again! But this time I wasn't being blamed. The mothers were blaming each other for a disastrous marriage which would surely only end in grief and apparently, God forbid, divorce, a mortal sin. According to Momma G., we were hedonistic pagans and her son's wedding wasn't even blessed by a priest.

Mother was screaming at her, calling her an ignorant peasant who believed in superstitious nonsense.

It was not going well. Tony and Lexi managed to pull away from their mothers and were backing out of the room. Their bags were packed and sitting by the door since they were leaving on their honeymoon in the morning.

"Come on," I whispered. They got their coats, and we snuck out the front door, running down to Dad's car. We jumped in and I fired it up, backing frantically down the driveway to head to the airport.

Our mothers appeared on the doorstep, shaking their fists at us. At least they weren't attacking each other. I saw my dad suddenly appear and Uncle Vinnie come from the garage apartment.

We drove in silence for a long while, when Tony said, "Well, at least I didn't burn the house down this time," and we laughed all the way to the airport.

Patti Gaustad Procopi is a former army brat who lived all over the world before settling in Gloucester, Virginia, with her husband Greg. They raised three daughters and numerous cats and dogs.

Patti worked at two area history museums for thirty-two years. After retiring, she finally had the time to do the thing she always wanted to do: write!

Patti's writing is about emotional connections, friendship and family. Her first novel, *Please…Tell Me More*, was published in 2020 by Blue Fortune Enterprises, LLC, followed by *I'll Get By*, *Stop Talking*, and *The Murderer You Know*, a podcast mystery.

Patti has had stories printed in literary journals and anthologies and read on a podcast. She's given talks at area libraries and writing symposiums about how to tell your story.

When not writing, Patti enjoys photographing birds on her creek. She also enjoys gardening, yoga, and researching her family genealogy.

You can find Patti's books on Barnes & Noble, Amazon, or wherever books are sold, and you can contact her on her website, pattiproauthor.com, or email patti.pro@cox.net or on Facebook.

A Debt Repaid

Bradley Harper

"Men's vows are women's traitors."
William Shakespeare
Cymbeline, act 3, scene 4

I believed him. I believed Master Jack when he promised my mother he'd care for me as well as have me tend to his baby daughter, Rosaline. We were bound for the New World, and it mattered not. I reckoned the rats there could be no worse than those who shared our home in London. I'd only been outside the city once, a year before, to help pick hops, and the thought of sailing across the world to a new land both thrilled and terrified me.

Life in Jamestown was hard, and food was scarce. Then winter came, and the food became scarcer still. Rosaline was listless as her mother's breasts ran dry, and we began eating the starch Master Jack had brought for his collars.

We were near six hundred souls when winter came. By New Year's, we were less than a third. Little Rosaline was barely one of the living. One night, as I shivered beneath my thin blanket, Master Jack returned from trading with the local Indians. He'd given them nearly everything made of iron save his ax, and I reckoned he'd surrendered that for a deer.

"Come with me to the stable, Sally," he said, and I supposed he needed help dressing the beast. I was near starving and sprang to follow, the promise of fresh meat giving me strength where there'd been none before. I stepped into the enclosure, but there was no carcass hanging from the ridgepole. I turned just in time to see the moon glint off the ax head… then darkness.

I went somewhere, my spirit hovering in a place neither near nor far, but with no map showing the way. My bones, picked clean, were dumped with those of other beasts, not in consecrated ground, but my soul refused to leave. The anger I felt at my betrayal became an anchor, and I remained. Angry. Vengeful. Patient. Time is nothing to the dead.

Jamestown faded into the marsh, forgotten for years, and I rested, uneasy, with the other spirits trapped in this folly of men's vanity.

Then a new age arrived, and the settlement was slowly restored, not to live in but as a display. A history lesson that taught the wrong lesson, praising the men who dragged me to a cold, unforgiving land. A place where the order of the Old World followed us to the New, and the strong used the weak for their ends.

The stars blazed overhead that night as I wandered along the shoreline. I heard a man's voice cursing, and I recognized a night watchman I sometimes followed as he made his rounds. I smelled his blood, fresh from the cut he'd suffered from a fall. It summoned me closer, and I recognized the aroma. It smelled of me. The moon was high, like the night my life ended, and in the pale light, I saw Master Jack's face reflected in the man's visage. Something of me resided in him, and I understood what the moonlight was trying to tell me.

My anger flamed, and I was given the power to reveal myself. I drove the screaming man into the water, and my ghostly companions, summoned by my wailing, surrounded his struggling form until he struggled no more.

I see him some nights, walking along the path he walked in life, and I give him free passage. His ancestor's debt is paid in full. The chains binding me here grow weaker, and soon my soul will make its final journey. I do not fear the judgment that awaits.

My anger has cooled, and I am at rest. Wherever I go from here, I am certain Master Jack will not be there to greet me.

Bradley Harper is a retired US Army physician who began writing after retirement. During his time serving in Colombia with US Special Forces, the FARC (the Revolutionary Armed Forces of Colombia) placed a $1.5 million bounty for his capture. (Offer no longer valid.)

Dr. Harper's debut novel, *A Knife in the Fog*, was a 2019 Edgars Finalist for Best First Novel by an American. The book won Killer Nashville's Silver Falchion award as Best Mystery, and the audiobook won Audiofile Magazine's Earphone award in the Mystery category. The book has been translated into Japanese and German and is a Recommended Read by the Arthur Conan Doyle estate.

The sequel, *Queen's Gambit*, won the 2020 Silver Falchion as Best Suspense and Book of the Year. His recently produced short animation, *Dark Tryst*, has won multiple awards across Europe. His poetry and essays have been published in various magazines. He recently co-wrote a memoir by Leslie Lautenslager, *My Time with Colin Powell*, about her twenty-five years as GEN Powell's personal assistant, and his detective story, *Reflections in a Dragon's Eye*, is a 2024 Finalist for the Silver Falchion Award.

Doctor Harper recently received his master's degree in creative writing from Napier University in Edinburgh. While residing in the UK, he was voted a Fellow of the Royal Scottish Society for the Arts after his presentation, "Sherlock Holmes as Science Fiction," detailing how Doyle's character inspired the world's first crime lab.

You can follow him on Facebook at Bradley Harper-Author, and on X (Twitter) @BHarperAuthor.

His website is www.BHarperAuthor.Com

The Window

ML Brei

Amy had always loved the house. When she saw it again with adult eyes, she could picture herself spending warm summer nights on the covered front porch, fans softly whirling overhead, she and her friends relaxing in the rocking chairs, enjoying iced tea.

The house had once belonged to her grandmother, a feisty woman who was constantly confronting something with a broom. Amy's family spent many holidays visiting her, especially after her grandfather died. She knew her grandfather only as a quiet man who couldn't quite remember who anybody was. When her grandfather died, her grandmother carried on as vigorously as ever, determined to stay in her home. After she died, the house sat empty and forlorn, slowly slipping into disrepair.

When Amy's mother and stepfather finally decided to renovate and refurbish the house, Amy jumped at the chance to live there and offered to rent it from them. But she had to wait as spring turned into summer and one project morphed into another. First, they tore out the old carpet throughout the house and refinished the fine oak floors underneath. They painted and freshened up the bedrooms and even installed a new roof. When the leaves on the trees started to turn, Amy decided it was time to move in, even though the renovations weren't complete. A hall bath and an upstairs bedroom were closed off and the exterior siding had yet to be replaced. That hardly mattered. She had three good-sized, freshly appointed bedrooms, a quaint family room, and more space than she needed. The house felt like hers. Mostly.

Shortly after she moved in, her roommate from college, Jen, contacted her with the surprising news that she would be moving into town. Did Amy have a spare room? Yes.

Jen, a tall, slender girl with short black hair and a no-nonsense approach to life, arrived shortly thereafter. "You moved in before they even finished the bathroom? It doesn't have a floor. Seriously, someone could fall through and break their neck." She dropped her backpack with a thud.

"That's okay. I usually keep the door closed. Just pretend it's not there. You can use the bathroom in my bedroom." Amy pulled the bathroom door shut firmly and opened another to reveal an old brass bed topped with a cornflower coverlet that matched the curtains. The room was sparsely furnished, stripped of any personal touches. A slipper chair with a matching pillow sat in one corner beside a highboy bureau whose surface remained pristine. The only sign of Amy's presence was the bedside table, where she kept her phone, a tangle of chargers, and a few scattered essentials. "I don't mind, really."

"Is that your grandmother's furniture?" Jen asked.

"Most of it. I love the old-fashioned feel, don't you? It transports me back to the colonial days. I mean, I like modern life, believe me, but living so close to the historic area and being in a colonial-ish house makes me feel as though I'm part of it. Right?"

Jen surveyed the room. There was a window on the back wall, a door to the bathroom and a long closet on a second wall. The third and adjacent fourth wall, however, were blank canvases of off-white save for an oval mirror and a landscape painting on the fourth wall. "It's nice, but it seems to be missing something," Jen said.

Amy followed Jen's glance. "Oh, yes, I see what you mean. Well, that's the way it's going to be. My stepdad doesn't like to hang anything on the walls. He has a thing about holes. Apparently it was expensive to have everything fixed up and painted."

Amy led her friend to the room across the hall. "This

is your room. What do you think? Isn't the canopy heavenly! Fair warning, the bed occasionally squeaks. You'll get used to it. I asked my stepdad to rejigger my bed so it doesn't make a sound. You know how I can't sleep through random noise. Your bed, however, is an old four-poster. It was always in the guest bedroom. It's got personality."

"Yeah. I like it," Jen said, fingering the lace fringe of the hanging.

"This house used to be so creaky! My grandmother always complained about random noises at night. She said the place needed buttoning up. So my stepdad 'buttoned' it up. Not sure what he did. But I have slept soundly from the very first night I moved in. Hope you do too! Much better than our dorm room, right? Go ahead and unpack. I'll be downstairs. As soon as you're settled, we'll head over to Colonial Williamsburg. It's fun to be there as the sun is setting. It is so cool. Everyone is dressed in period clothing and they talk with an accent. You'll love it!"

The street was nearly deserted as twilight descended, surrounding the two young women in long shadows and a golden glow as they strolled past silent brick and wood-shingled houses and shops: the silversmith, the milliner, the grocer. A long, narrow stack of split firewood formed a low wall in front of the Prentis store. They briefly stopped in front of the eighteenth-century courthouse before continuing to a moss-covered low brick wall, which surrounded a church with white-framed Palladian windows and an octagonal spire. The church was surrounded by an ancient graveyard of memorials, crumbling gravestones, and trees heavily laden with golden and rust-colored leaves. The tall red gates were propped open.

"Perfect. It's still open. Welcome to Bruton Parish! It's from before the Revolution, but it is still as church as church could be! To me, this is the heart of this place. This is where is gets interesting."

Jen, dragging her feet as she followed a bouncy Amy through the open gates, eyed the spire and the front entrance.

"I'll take you inside some other time," Amy said over her shoulder. "Come, I want to show you my favorites."

Jen dutifully followed, staring straight ahead. The air had become chilly. "Brrr, is it haunted?" she asked.

Amy laughed, her reddish-brown curls dancing. "This place is at least 300 years old. It'd be odd if it weren't, right?"

Jen drew back. "I don't do ghost stories. Let the dead stay dead."

"Ah, but for every stone, every grave marker, there's a story, right? Just think, this place is thick with memories, Jen. Look around, can't you feel it?" Amy's voice lowered. "Maybe they're dead now, but once they breathed; they wandered this ground. And are they really gone?" Amy glanced at Jen, who was looking distinctly glum.

Amy recognized her friend's discomfort. "Okay! I'll spare you my favorites. But… don't look too closely at that one over there." She pointed to a tall, weathered granite obelisk, leaning slightly to its side, moss and lichen-covered. "You might see the anguished face of a woman, consumed with madness, screeching at a man whose own face was never found. He's down there somewhere, lurking," Amy said in a hushed tone.

Jen glanced toward the obelisk for a brief second and then at Amy.

Amy put her hands in front of her face. "Don't look back! She only stares if you notice," Amy said, hiding a smile.

Jen shuddered. "Stop it! You're giving me the chills."

Amy continued along the path through the graveyard and pointed down. "They say that something mysterious was buried and hidden beneath this very ground, and the only way to access it is through a secret tunnel under the Wren Building on the campus. Twenty years ago, it was all over the local newspaper. I remember my grandmother reading it to me."

Jen took a deep breath.

Amy saw her friend stiffen. She laughed and gave her a hug. "Okay, no more stories. I promise. Let's head back. We'll explore more next time."

When they got home from their excursion, they ordered a pizza and bundled in blankets on the front porch, chatting and listening to music. The moon was a small waxing crescent and the stars were plentiful on this peaceful autumn evening.

When the conversation had run its course at a late hour, they said goodnight.

Jen closed the guest room door firmly. Finally alone, her mouth curved slightly when she saw the four-poster bed. She slipped under the cotton sheets and duvet. The mattress was perfect. The fancy lace canopy overhead made her feel as though she were in a five-star hotel. She closed her eyes with a contented sigh and started to drift off. All was silent and peaceful.

Not awake, yet not asleep, she thought she heard a dull groan of a floorboard. No, a creak. Was a floorboard creaking or disintegrating? Or failing? She imagined in her mind's eye the bathroom floor with rotten floorboards. She turned to the other side and slipped back into a haze. In this dream-like state, a muffled clang of a pipe. Then silence. A drip. Nothing. A rustling. Tense quiet. A different floorboard? Splintering. A body falling through? Then a hush. At last, the slow rasp of a sash lifting.

Jen's eyes flew open and her heart pounded. She grabbed the duvet and thrust it over her head. Taking deep breaths, she counted backwards as she faded into a troubled sleep.

"It's really a noisy house at night," Jen said as Amy drove the two of them to a pumpkin patch the next morning, a sunny yet chilly Saturday.

"You think so? Funny. I haven't heard anything. But I haven't slept in the guest bedroom since the renovation. You think it's your bed?"

"My bed? No. My bed's perfect. Just a bunch of weird noises. Something near the hall bath? The floor, you know…"

"No, that floor may look like it's about to fall in, but I've walked on it and I'm here, the floor's there."

"But then it sounded as though you opened a window."

Amy turned and glanced at her, raised an eyebrow, and returned her eyes to the road. "Why would I do that?"

"Well, that's what it sounded like. That's all."

"You have a vivid imagination."

They spent a good portion of the morning dashing around the pumpkin patch as though they were little kids trying to find the most perfect pumpkin ever.

When they finally returned home, they lugged half a dozen pumpkins of various sizes and shapes, all perfect, to the front porch and arranged them. Once inside, Amy plunked bunches of autumn flowers, chrysanthemums, zinnias, celosia, wheatgrass, and several large late-blooming sunflowers, onto the kitchen counter. She systematically tipped the stems and removed greenery from each, then thoughtfully arranged a grouping in a vase. The rest were wrapped in paper. Gathering the bundle in her hand, she waltzed over to Jen.

"Want to come with?" she asked.

"Where?"

"I want to take these to my grandmother's grave. Look, aren't they perfect for Halloween?"

Jen considered the flowers for a moment, then shook her head. "I don't need to go back to that creepy graveyard."

Amy laughed. "She's not at Bruton. She and my grandfather are at Cedar Grove, about a mile from here. It's open and like a park. Nothing creepy, I promise. It's a nice walk."

Jen agreed and the two set off. As Amy promised, the cemetery was a large, open area, dotted with mature cedars throughout. A narrow lane looped around the different sections of the cemetery. The memorials and gravestones were upright and clean. Benches and watering stations were thoughtfully placed.

"Yes, this is better," Jen said.

At one point the path joined a low brick wall, similar to those in the historic district, that enclosed older, crumbling gravestones. Jen walked briskly by.

Before they reached their destination, Amy stopped to fill a watering can. She handed it to Jen. "Do you mind?"

"Not at all."

They continued until they reached an impressive double gravestone of granite with built-in flower holders at each end. The etching of the names and dates was clean and sharp. Without a word, Amy went to one end, reached into a vase, and pulled out a plastic liner. She shook out the debris. After filling it with water and flowers, she repeated the process at the other end, then stood back to assess her work.

"My grandmother loved flowers. Always had fresh arrangements in the house. Wouldn't allow anything artificial. She chose this gravestone before my grandfather died. She wanted to be united with him in every sense of the word. I didn't really know my grandfather, but I'm sure he was incredible; she was always talking about him. But the funniest thing, even after he was gone, she worried about him. A bit whacky, right? But so kind to me. So, I come here every once in a while to bring her flowers."

"That's very thoughtful," Jen said.

Amy fell silent. Jen looked down at the grass. She spotted a small greenish-gray, shimmery rock, and nudged it loose with her shoe.

"What's that?" Amy said, catching the movement of Jen's foot.

Jen stooped down and carefully pulled out a small object encrusted in the dirt.

Amy leaned over. "How unusual. Shaped like a heart!"

Jen examined it closely, turned it over, and back again. "Look at the little crystals… deep red. I wonder if they're garnet."

"Garnet. You mean the gemstone garnet? Oh, that's funny! Or a coincidence. My grandmother always said that my grandfather was a rockhound. He loved rocks and gemstones. Apparently he found them all the time. Just as you did. They were everywhere in the house. I remember the crystals they kept on the mantel. When my grandmother turned on the spotlight, they danced. It seemed magical to me, and I always wanted to play with them. Once I went into his office and he showed me rows and rows of different colors and shapes of rocks neatly lined up. I can just imagine how thrilled he'd be! Good eyes, Jen!"

Later that night, Jen looked at the rock again. She had washed it, and the little crystals now dazzled. She placed it on the dressing table in her bedroom and then thought of other things, such as whether she'd get decent sleep that night. She sat on the bed and bounced on it lightly. It creaked distinctly, but it was a different sound from what she heard the previous night. She strode heavily around the bed, testing the floorboards. They seemed sound. Then, she quietly tiptoed down to the hall bathroom and opened the door. It looked as it had the day before. She decided that her sleepless night was a fluke.

As she slipped into sleep, the far-off whistle of a train

pierced the stillness. A few minutes later, a floorboard creaked. She held her breath. Another creak. She waited for it. The slow rasping sound of wood against wood. She pictured in her mind a window rising slowly. *It couldn't be*, she thought. But then it was complete silence, a void. She didn't move a muscle until at last sleep overtook her.

The next morning was a gray and moody Sunday. Both women slept in late. Jen was first down for breakfast and started the coffee. As she groggily poured cereal into a bowl, Amy bellowed from the stairs, "Thanks for the heart!"

Jen retrieved a milk carton from the refrigerator. "What?" she yelled over her shoulder as she continued to prepare her breakfast. Amy appeared at the kitchen door and held the rock out to Jen.

"That was sweet! But you dug it out of the ground. You should keep it. I would never have noticed it."

"What?" Jen repeated and glanced at Amy's outstretched hand cradling the heart rock.

"Your heart rock. I found it on my bureau, you know, the one right next to the window. Didn't you put it there?" She showed Jen the rock.

"No, I left it on my dresser."

Amy cocked her head to one side with a quizzical look on her face. "Are you sure?"

"Of course."

"Okay. Let's check it out." She turned and dashed up the stairs to Jen's room and returned a few seconds later.

Jen poured coffee for the two of them.

"Well, your dresser is completely clear. No rock. How odd. Here, this is yours, obviously." Amy held it out.

Jen accepted the rock. "Yes, very odd," she said. "If anyone had moved it, I'd know. I heard sounds in the house again last night. I had a terrible time falling asleep. It started with the train."

"How'd you hear that? We're a couple miles from the train station."

"I don't know, but after the train, the floorboards started. At least I think it was the floorboards. It sounded like creaking floorboards. And if that weren't enough, the window opened again. I swear it sounded like a window was opening."

"Did you check your windows? Maybe the top sash slips down when the atmospheric pressure changes."

"Does that happen?"

"Maybe?"

They finished their breakfast. After Jen returned the rock to her dresser, they inspected the two windows in her bedroom. Both were solid and fit snugly within their frames. The women concluded that the sashes couldn't have moved on their own or because of any change in air pressure. Next they checked Amy's window, which was secured with a key lock. Amy glanced around until she spotted a small key on a hook at the side of the window frame. It too hadn't been opened for a while.

That evening, they decided to switch rooms.

"Sorry you'll be kept up tonight," Jen said to Amy as they swapped pillows. "But you'll have a better chance of identifying the source of the sounds."

"Sure, no problem. I'll listen very attentively. See, I have my notepad. I'll make notes and report back in the morning." They laughed and said goodnight.

Amy tucked herself into bed and checked to see that her flashlight, notepad, and pencil were within reach. She turned on a little book light, then opened a book. Before long, she was fast asleep.

Jen, meanwhile, surveyed her new surroundings and with a satisfied look on her face, snuggled under the covers, content with the world.

Then, an ever so soft, gentle tread outside the door. She took a deep breath. Silence. Something skittered overhead. She braced herself, anticipating what would come next. A floorboard creaked, then a long period of silence. Another floorboard. A soft rasping of wood against wood as the window sash slowly slid past the frame. Her heart raced. She reached for the lamp switch and light flooded the room.

Everything looked in order. The window was closed. Nothing was amiss. She shook her head. As she reached to turn off the lamp, something caught her eye on top of the bureau. She stared at it for a moment, forcing her eyes to focus, then recognized the small object: her heart-rock. She looked at the lamp. Her hand hovered then withdrew, leaving the light burning through the night.

The next morning, as Jen recounted the events of the night before, Amy just threw her hands in the air.

"It's uncanny! I don't know what you're hearing. I didn't hear a thing," she said. "Slept like a baby." She thrust her blank notepad toward Jen. "See, no notes. Nothing to report." Then she stopped for a moment before continuing. "Maybe it doesn't matter. I just got a message from my stepdad. The people who are changing out the siding start work today and guess what—they'll be cutting through my wall, you know the long blank wall, to install a second window."

"Oh, that makes a lot of sense. That's what's missing."

"Yes. However, it means that we'll have to bunk downstairs for a few days. They'll be in and out upstairs. My mom thinks it'll be best if we clear out until the work is done. I think it'll be fun, kind of like camping but without the stars. It's too cold to camp outdoors anyway."

"Got it."

Jen sat down and put the heart rock on the counter. "By any chance, did you put my rock on your bureau yesterday?"

"Not again! I haven't touched it."

"I didn't think so." Jen's gaze drifted across the kitchen to the mantel above the fireplace in the family room. A few decorative items were arranged around an old Seth Thomas clock.

"I know what I'll do," she said. With long, purposeful strides, she walked to the mantel and placed the rock next to an abstract bronze figurine of an angel. "Let's give this rock a new home."

"It looks perfect there," Amy said.

The work on the siding of the house took a good part of the week. By Friday, the job was completed, and Amy and Jen moved back upstairs to their rooms.

"Look at all this light… it's so open and airy!" Amy beamed as she swirled around the room. "It's a completely different room! I love it."

Jen nodded. "This is exactly what it needed."

That night, after a long evening entertaining friends, the women retired later than usual. Jen was exhausted and decided that she was not going to tolerate random noises disrupting her sleep. She carried earplugs, an eye mask, a flashlight, and a small cast-iron skillet to bed. Just in case.

Without another thought, she nodded off and remained so long and deep. No groans from a floorboard or pipe or window sash. No train whistles, no skittering overhead. The house was silent. The next morning, as the sun rose above the horizon, Jen woke up a very refreshed person.

When Jen told Amy she hadn't heard anything the night before, Amy let out a sigh of relief. "Who would've thought adding a window would help button-up the house," she said.

Several months later, Amy and Jen revisited Jen's first few nights in the house. "Funny conversation with my mom yesterday," Amy said. "I wanted to know why they added another window to my bedroom. So I asked her. And you know what she said?"

"They wanted more light?"

"No. It was my grandfather's idea. Apparently, he always wanted another window in that room. My grandmother, however, wouldn't have it. As it was, she was terrified that he would open the window one night and fall out. So, she always kept it locked and hid the key."

"Why would she think that?"

"He sleepwalked and did the strangest things in his sleep."

About the Author

ML Brei is an accomplished writer, teacher, consultant, and small business owner. She is the author of several books including *A Different Type of Soul* (2022, Meripoint Books), *The Christian Symbols of the Twelve Days of Christmas* (2022, Meripoint Books), and *Forever Stage IV* (2023, Meripoint Books).

She is a graduate of Smith College and has three grown children. After living abroad for many years as a military spouse, she now resides in Virginia with her husband of 38 years. ML can be reached through her publisher, meripointbooks.com.

The Piggly Wiggly Parking Lot Was A Portal

Lissette Lorenz

The Piggly Wiggly on Princess Anne Road sat like a relic of a time that refused to die. Mr. Pig, the grocery chain's mascot, smiled benevolently from his perch above the sliding glass doors, his bright cartoon eyes wide and gleaming beneath the streetlights.

Zizi could feel the pig's gaze as she sat in the driver's seat of her rusty red 2001 Toyota Corolla. Steering wheel in a death grip, chest heaving, she found herself praying to Mr. Pig again.

Please can you stop the noise...please can you stop the noise...please can you...

Once the floodgates opened like this, there was no stopping it. The storm of sensory overload simply had to run its course. If only she wasn't in public. She hated when her episodes happened in public. But it was precisely in public when she was most susceptible to them. "Autistic meltdowns," her therapist called them. Not tantrums, like her schoolteachers said back in the day, to the consternation of her parents and the ridicule of her peers.

What a supermassive weirdo…

At least the parking lot was empty. Even the last-minute candy shoppers were already back on their porches, ready for the next greedy ghoul or goblin to come traipsing up their driveways. Droves of children with chonky cheeks had taken over the streets since well before sunset, high on high-fructose corn syrup and Acid Yellow 23 food coloring.

In the Corolla, overwhelming sensations crashed down in sheets across Zizi's body, thoughts crackling like lightning in quick succession.

…après moi le deluge…

Mayday, mayday! I repeat—

Abort the mission! I repeat! Abort the mission!

This sure makes you look pretty ugly…

The veins in Zizi's arms buzzed painfully. When the meltdowns got this bad, it always felt as though giant interdimensional mosquitoes were sucking out her life force from the crooks of her arms. What was that grounding technique that Dr. Li had taught her last week?

Set your feet firmly on the floor and wiggle your toes. She pushed through the barrage of intrusive thoughts she had battled since childhood. Blinked through the tears. Wiped the snot onto her sleeve of her orange plaid shirt. Looked down at her dirty hand-me-down tennies and the car's dusty carpet. The floormat was caked with dried mud and pine needles. Greenish-tinged loblolly pollen from two seasons ago still clung to its edges.

Take deep breaths and count down from ten. She forced herself to peel her hands off the steering wheel, already missing the pressure she had applied to it, the birth squeeze of leathery plastic on skin, and placed her palms face-down on her lap. She trembled.

Count down from ten. A flash and then—

Ten-nine-eight-seven-six-five—

We knew the world would never be the same…

…the panic, the vomit, the—

…the dust and the screaming—

Some people laughed. A few people cried. Most were silent…

Breathe, Zizi, breathe. Breathe, Zizi—

Four-three-two-one—

"Zizi."

The last voice did not seem to come from the inside of Zizi's skull. It came from the empty passenger seat. Except it was no longer empty.

The Being beside Zizi shimmered. They looked

human at first. Then they didn't. Their features flowed like mercury, refracting back Zizi's face and then fragmenting into something else. Their skin glimmered like stars through fog. Their eyes were like three voids, terrifying and comforting all at once. When Zizi looked into the being's eyes, all the voices, all the noise, all the sensory static, suddenly stopped.

Being spoke again.

"Zizi, it's time."

"Are you real?"

Being smiled. "Are *you?*"

"Of course you chose tonight." Zizi's voice was hoarse, exhausted from all the sobbing that had only just subsided, thanks to this being. "All the freaks are free to walk the Earth tonight without suspicion. Even me. Even you."

"Yes, the veil is thinnest now. Between their world and ours. Between your thoughts and your origins."

"I've been losing my mind," Zizi confessed. The episodes, these "meltdowns," had been becoming increasingly frequent. And for some strange reason, it had only been in this parking lot, under Mr. Pig's bizarrely benevolent gaze, where she seemed to find a shred of respite, however temporary. And now here she was in the parking lot, in her beat-up Toyota, with Being sort of sit-hovering beside her.

Being spoke again. Zizi found herself floating once

more in their triad of voids-for-eyes. "You are awakening."

Zizi looked away and felt all the familiar pain seep back into her pores. "To what? To the fact that I'm a nutcase? That I have a broken brain? That I'm a broken human?" Zizi fought back the urge to cry. Again.

"No. To your *design*." Being leaned in. "Zizi, you are not human. You are a bio-synthetic intelligence encased in human form. You were placed here on Earth by a council of civilizations beyond your stars. Your kind were scattered across this planet to help Earth transition to the phase of her evolution before Homo sapiens could destroy her. This species' intelligence has yet to surpass their older hierarchical instincts. They needed guidance."

"But how was I supposed to know what to do if I didn't know all this? If I didn't know my purpose? If I didn't even know what I was?"

"You couldn't know. All of that was part of your construction. We hoped you would trust your programming. Empathize with humans. Live like them. Believe you were one yourself. The mission required this to be so. If you knew, if they knew, they'd try to disassemble you and destroy us. And while they are incapable of doing that, they do have the capacity to destroy themselves, and planet Earth with them."

"Well," sighed Zizi, "we seem to be failing in our mission. World War Three feels just around the corner. Look who has access to the codes these days! Meanwhile, look at me. I can't even manage to get myself to stop shopping at the Piggly Wiggly. And I'm a vegan!"

Being laughed, a sound at once beautiful and tragic. "That's the contradiction of the human condition. You seem to have learned it from them. With enough exposure, you come to love the very things you were meant to hate."

Zizi tilted her head skyward and closed her eyes, finally able to take that deep breath that had eluded her earlier. This whole cosmic drama was just… too much. She couldn't decide whether to laugh or to cry. *I guess I could do both.* She felt grateful that her programming had granted her the ability to do so. *I guess I have Being to thank for that kindness.* She turned to face the passenger seat.

But when she opened her eyes, Being was gone. It was just Zizi and Mr. Pig again.

God loves his children…

God loves his children, yeah…

About the Author

Lissette Lorenz creates speculative fabulations at the intersection of art, science, and the environment. Their work can be found in *Art + Media: Journal of Art and Media Studies*, *JCOM: Journal of Science Communication*, and Objet-a Creative Studio's *BECOMING* trilogy.

Using mixed media, they blend poetry, prose, zine-making, and collage to explore themes of Earthly un/worlding during times of planetary transition. Lissette was born and raised in Miami, Florida, a bioregion that has been transformed from Everglades wetland to teetering metropolis.

A child of Latin American immigrants fleeing war and poverty, they grew up somewhere between princess-like Disney World fantasies and complicated post-colonial realities. They also lived in Tokyo, New York City, and New Orleans before settling in Virginia Beach with their partner and many, many plants. Find more at lissettelorenz.com.

The Guardian

Narielle Living

She hadn't been able to wash the taste of dirt out of her mouth. Or the particles of soil and who knew what else out of her mop of short red hair. Of course, that's what happens when a person face-plants on a dusty road while trying to outrun some weird creature that wanted… what did it want? Her soul? Or only her body? Whatever it wanted, she wasn't giving it away.

She dropped her head into her hands, tired of looking at her laptop screen, tired of trying to find answers. Just tired. *Come on, Nyx, pull it together*, she thought. *You're imagining things.*

A wet nose pushed into her face, nudging her and bringing a smile. Nyx reached out and hugged her dog. "Thanks, Siggy. You're amazing." The yellow butt wiggled while Siggy sniffed her up and down, as if trying to figure out if something was wrong.

Nyx slowly ran her hand down the dog's head, taking comfort as the yellow lab leaned against her. "Nothing wrong except I was chased today by a man who turned into an animal and tried to kill me." She laughed, the sound sharp and barking, as if she wasn't used to laughing anymore. "Either I'm losing it or I have the worst luck with dating."

It was supposed to be a date of sorts. Someone she'd met at the gym, exchanged glances with, texted a few times. Tall, slicked-back dark hair, muscled but not overly muscled. Handsome, with a great sense of humor.

How could it have gone so wrong so quickly?

Of course there was always the possibility that she was crazy, that she had imagined everything and maybe scared him off with her insanity. She had shown up at the restaurant near Colonial Williamsburg where they were supposed to meet, dressed for both comfort and allure in her black leather jacket, black jeans, and blue silk top. Before she could step inside, she heard it. Her sister. "Nyx… please… help me…" But it couldn't be her sister, because her sister had been dead for three years.

"Please… I'm here. I'm right here."

Of course she went around the side of the building, where there was nothing but deep puddles from the recent torrential downpour and a dumpster overflowing with a strange assortment of tree limbs, clothing, and furniture.

"Helen?" she had called, deeply uneasy and uncertain of what was happening. Someone was playing a joke or she was mistaking another woman's cries for those of her sister.

Then it stepped out from behind the dumpster. The hair was still slicked back but he had changed. His shoulders were broader, his hair had grown. Sweat ran down his face and steam drifted off his chest, as if he were overheating.

An animal growl erupted from somewhere.

Nyx did not wait to find out what that growling meant. She knew without being told that he would hurt her. Kill, maim, whatever. She wasn't waiting around to find out.

Nothing good ever happens next to a dumpster, she thought with rising hysteria. Time to go.

She ran without thought, without a plan. She zigzagged through the streets, making turns and running through the front door of one store and out the rear, trying to lose him. Hopping a bus that had just pulled up to the corner—because there was no way she was going to wait for a ride—she rode until it brought her to the edge of town. Lackey. She cut through the neighborhood across from the Naval Weapons Station, darting behind trees and trying not to cry.

She had to be quiet. Nobody could hear her.

She finally made her way to the edge of the woods, property owned by the water company, and she ran. She knew these woods well, had played in them years ago when she was growing up. Home was close.

Halfway through the woods, she stopped. What if he had found out where she lived? What if he was waiting for her—in her house, in her room?

She began shivering, unable to stop. *This is ridiculous. I just need to get home.* An image of her dog rose in her mind, and she calmed. She would be safe at home.

Moving quickly but now trying to be quiet, she half jogged to her yard, watching her surroundings to make sure she wasn't being followed. Her home was on a corner lot, a small, two-story house that had been built in the early 1900s. Her family had lived there for generations, and as the structure came into view, a bark sounded.

Siggy, sitting in the front yard, waiting for her.

Maybe he hadn't actually shifted into a scary monster guy. Maybe he was sitting in his apartment somewhere wondering what the hell just happened and if his date had totally lost her mind.

Or maybe this was what her grandmother, Molly, had warned her about.

She returned her attention to her laptop screen and closed it. Nothing she read was going to help. Her phone, sitting on the table, buzzed. It was a text from Belinda, her best friend since sixth grade.

You ok?

Nyx hesitated. Was she okay? How could she describe her evening to her BFF via text? Was there an emoji for this? Simple is best, she thought.

Yep. I'm good.

No ur not, Belinda answered. *I'm coming over.*

Nyx was not going to argue with her. It would be good to have a friend right now. Siggy, lying on his side at her feet, whined. "Another friend," she clarified to the dog. "Because you are the bestest boy ever."

It only took Belinda ten minutes, probably because she always drove too fast. She didn't knock because she hadn't knocked on Nyx's door since she was a kid asking Nyx's mom if she could come out and play.

"What happened?" Belinda demanded, walking into the kitchen with her blonde hair piled on top of her head, wearing pajama bottoms and a hoodie and plunking her bag onto the kitchen table as she slid into a chair.

"I don't really know how to say this." Nyx stood and refilled her water glass. "Do you want something?"

"I have an energy drink." She pulled the bottle from her bag and waved it at Nyx. "I want you to tell me what happened."

She took a deep breath and tried to organize her thoughts. "Okay, but what I am going to tell you is… difficult. I'm not even sure I know what is true anymore."

Belinda stood. "Did he hurt you?"

Nyx shook her head. "No. Let's go into the living room. The couch is more comfortable, and this might take a minute to explain."

It took longer than a minute. It took almost twenty minutes, because Nyx was trying to recall the exact order of things and be precise with her description, and of course Belinda had questions. Lots of questions.

At the end, Belinda sat back on the couch, a thoughtful expression on her face. "Let me make sure I've got this," she said. "You were supposed to have a date with a man who sort of shape-shifted into a weird otter kind of thing and chased you through Williamsburg until you were able to elude him by hopping on a bus and running home once you got off in Lackey. You're not sure what he wanted but you assume he wanted to… kill you?"

Nyx shook her head. "Not exactly kill. It wasn't anything he said, but it felt like he wanted to… destroy me?"

"And how is that different from killing you?"

"Yeah, sounds similar, but the difference is that killing means you get to be dead, which leads to tunnels and light and reincarnation and all the things that go with being dead. Destroying means you get none of that. You don't return to the wheel of life, your soul is crushed, and you cease to exist in any form." Nyx took a deep breath, trying to stop the feeling that ice had lodged in her center. The thought of being annihilated was just a wee bit overwhelming. Her voice shook as she added, "Plus there was Helen's voice. It used my sister's voice."

Belinda leaned forward and put her hand on Nyx's arm. "You know who we have to talk to, right? There's only one person who can help us with this."

Nyx smiled. "Thank you for saying 'us' and for not thinking I'm crazy."

"I don't think you're crazy," Belinda said. "I think your family is crazy."

Nyx laughed. "Then let's go see Grandma tomorrow. We'll bring her a pumpkin spice latte. It is October, after all." Siggy, sprawled on the floor near the couch, gave a dog sigh and stretched. "You can come too, Sig. They love seeing you there."

"That's only because you tell them that he's a therapy dog," Belinda protested. "He is so not a therapy dog."

"He's better than a therapy dog," Nyx exclaimed.

"I agree." Belinda nodded. "He is so much more than that. But he hasn't gone through the training and he doesn't have the papers—"

"Grandma will never tell," Nyx said. "She loves Siggy. I think they have some kind of psychic connection."

Belinda stood and walked toward the kitchen. "Now I'm going to raid your refrigerator for the half-empty bottle of white wine you have in there. And of course your grandmother and your dog are connected. Ever since I've known you, your family has had some variation of a dog that looks like Siggy."

Siggy sat up, panting, and stared at Belinda as she walked away. "No offense, Sig," Belinda called over her shoulder. "But there has been a floofy yellow dog here for a long time, which would indicate that your type has taken up permanent residence here at Nyx's house since... forever."

Siggy woofed and padded after her into the kitchen.

Reluctantly, Nyx followed. Her body ached and she was in no mood for alcohol. "Are you guessing that I have wine in the fridge?" she asked as Belinda stood staring into the recesses of her refrigerator.

"You always have an open bottle of wine. You open a bottle and you never finish it."

Nyx had to admit that was true. "What time can you go tomorrow?"

Belinda shuddered. "What time does that horrible place start allowing visitors?"

The horrible place she was referring to was the assisted living facility her mother had chosen for her grandmother. Several years ago, her mother had started hinting things like, "Your grandmother seems to be rather forgetful lately. I'm worried she will leave the stove on and the house will burn down." (Her grandmother, Molly, a free spirit, was only forgetful when her mother tried to corner her into doing things like playing bridge or having lunch with people she thought of as boring.) Her not-so-favorite conversation was when her mother said, "I don't know why your grandmother insists on talking about the old ways and spirits and all that airy-fairy stuff. It's embarrassing. I think it's a sign of dementia." (Molly had always talked about this kind of thing and it had always driven her mother batty. Her mother did not believe in what she couldn't see but Molly always told Nyx it didn't change what was there anyway and it didn't change who their family was. When Nyx asked who their family was, she would smile and avoid answering.)

Nyx wasn't sure why her grandmother caved and moved into the facility, but she did so only with the stipulation that Nyx live in her home, the house that had been in their family for generations. Belinda and she made it a point to spend time with Molly as much as they could, taking her out for ice cream or to the movies or lunch or anywhere but that place. It wasn't a bad place, but it certainly didn't reflect her grandmother's vibrant personality.

"How about we take her out for an early breakfast tomorrow, so you and I can be on time for work?"

Belinda nodded. "That works for me. I don't have to start until late morning anyway. In the meantime, are we staying at my house or yours?"

Her throat burned, and she stared at her friend, unable to form the words of gratitude.

"Let's stay here," Belinda said, taking a last swallow of her wine. "You and Sig can ride to my place with me and help me get my stuff."

"Thank you," Nyx said quietly. "I am grateful—"

"Yeah, yeah, friendship. You'd do the same thing for me." Not one for overt displays of emotion, ever, Belinda smiled. "Ready?"

"Why stay here? What about your place?"

Belinda's face hardened. "Because if he's coming for you, we want to know. He'll probably try something tonight, maybe tomorrow. Guys like that don't like to be told 'no'. I'll pack enough stuff for a few days. I'm not leaving you alone to face that… thing."

Siggy whined and pushed her head into Belinda's leg. "You're welcome," Belinda whispered.

Dragging her grandmother out of the assisted living facility at seven a.m. was more fun than she expected. Not so much for the people who worked there.

"Are we going to see the QUEEN?" Molly shouted as they walked toward the door, her short gray hair in spikes and her bedazzled jean jacket sparkling. "Can I have ice cream? With hot fudge?"

The nurse who accompanied them looked at Nyx and Belinda. "She's a bit confused this morning," she said in a low tone, as if her grandmother had lost her hearing.

"Perhaps we don't want to keep her out too long."

"What?" Nyx said. "It's hard to hear you when you whisper."

"Do you want sprinkles with your breakfast?" Belinda asked.

"*We* will be out for a while," Nyx said to the nurse. "Don't wait up!"

"She needs to be back by lunchtime," the woman sniffed. "It is important to maintain our schedule."

"It's your schedule, not mine," her grandmother said.

"Now Molly, you know we need to keep to our schedule," the nurse said.

Her grandmother shot her middle finger up at the nurse as they walked out the door. "Let's go home," she said to Nyx. "We can talk better in privacy."

Nyx and Belinda exchanged a look. Apparently Grandma knew they needed to talk, and she knew it was not something that could be made public.

At the house, Nyx made a pot of coffee, and they settled in the kitchen with a plate of homemade peanut butter brownies on the table. Siggy lay under the table, her head resting on Nyx's feet.

Grandma wasted no time. She folded her hands on the kitchen table and said, "Tell me what is going on."

Nyx did not hesitate. She started at the beginning and described meeting this man at the gym, flirting and talking, then the fateful night they were set to have a date. "I don't understand what I saw," Nyx said. "One moment I was excited to meet this new person, the next he was… morphing into some kind of… creature. And Helen. I heard Helen." She looked at her grandmother and hesitated. "You knew."

Her grandmother nodded. "What did he call himself this time?"

"He said his name was Kush. I assumed it was a family name or maybe reflected his heritage…"

Her grandmother gave a short, bitter laugh. "Yes, I suppose you could say it reflects his heritage. Kush is short for Kushtaka. Although these beings have also gone by other names, such as Wendigo. Some say even Saci and Kokopelli are relatives."

"Wait, what?" Belinda tilted her head, clearly confused. "What does that mean? I don't understand these names."

"It means I was hunted by something that was not quite human," Nyx said. "Which we already knew. I mean, humans don't generally go around shifting into otherworldly beings."

"Unless they have an endocrine disorder," Belinda said.

"Or a hormonal imbalance," Nyx acknowledged.

Her grandmother frowned. "This is serious. We must not lose sight of that." She leaned back and wrapped her hands around her coffee mug, looking directly at Nyx. "For your entire life, your mother forbade me from talking to you about this. She said that it was nonsense, that I was an imaginative old lady and shouldn't fill your head with lies."

Nyx let out a frustrated sigh. "I love Mom, I really do, but she's not… grounded in the same reality as we are. She is a 'what you see is what you get' kind of person. And even if I were more like her, last night certainly would have changed my worldview." She reached for a brownie and bit into it, taking a moment to savor the blend of chocolate and peanut butter, her favorites. "I have a feeling you know what this man-thing is."

Belinda took a brownie as well. "Nyx, I love your baking." She hesitated before taking a bite, looking at Molly. "Okay, so has this monster-beast been harassing you too?" She glanced at Nyx. "It obviously hasn't bothered your mom."

Both Nyx and Molly gave a short laugh. "Can you imagine?" Nyx said. "My mother would have that thing in a new hairstyle and new clothes and learning to speak proper English instead of growling."

Molly nodded in agreement. "Oh, that would be something to see." She sipped her coffee, put the mug on the table, and looked at Nyx. "But your mother is aware of all this. She has been warned, she simply chose to turn away from her heritage. This being has stalked our family for centuries. It knows our family, which is probably why it chose to use Helen's voice. It knows us."

"What?" Nyx yelled. "Why? Do we have to kill it?"

Molly shook her head. "No. It chooses one member of our family every twenty to thirty years. I have no idea why. Maybe because we can connect with the spirit world? I'm not sure if it goes after everyone or only us. The good news is that you don't have to kill it—I'm not even sure this thing could be killed. You simply have to defeat it for it to leave you alone."

"How the heck is she supposed to do that?" Belinda demanded. "It growled at her and shifted into a big, scary animal. Does she need to shoot it?"

Nyx dropped her head into her hands and gave a short wail. "I can't shoot at something! I'll end up missing or shooting the wrong thing and I'll go to jail."

Molly patted her arm. "No, dear, I wouldn't recommend you shoot at anything. When it came for me, I used fire and defeated it. Others in our family have simply avoided it. And the good news is that there is a time limit. This being only comes for us during October and the first week of November. Usually, if we can make it past November 1, we are safe."

"And it doesn't come back? It only comes for us once?" Nyx asked in a small voice. Seriously, she was all about otherworldly ghosts and beings and stuff, but being hunted by something like this was not on her bucket list.

Molly reached for a napkin and took a brownie, placing it on the napkin and breaking it into four pieces.

"Hmmmm… well…"

Nyx leaned forward and spoke slowly. "Grandma. Tell. Me. Right. Now. What's the deal?" Siggy stretched under the table, pressing his paw against her leg.

Moments passed. The grandfather clock ticked in the other room. Outside, a lawnmower started in the neighbor's yard. Finally, Molly said, "Here's what I know. Our family has been pitted against these shapeshifters for centuries. I'm not clear how it started, but my grandmother seemed to think it was because we stood up to them at some point, challenged their particular brand of evil."

Belinda snorted. "Sounds about right. You are both always on the side of justice for people, especially people who have been marginalized. I'll bet your ancestors did some sort of 'leave that kid alone' kind of thing and pissed off the shapeshifters and they're probably holding a grudge."

Molly nodded. "That about sums it up. A centuries-long grudge. I have no idea why they only come after us during the months of October and November, though, and I have no idea why they leave us alone the rest of the year."

"I have a theory." Nyx finished her coffee and stood, crossing the kitchen to get more. "October is Halloween, which we know is a time when we are more easily able to see the other side." She grabbed dog treats from the counter, returned to the table, and sat down, passing a treat to Siggy. "Talk to the ghosts, the ancestors, that kind of thing. The Day of the Dead is November 1, right? So after that, I assume the veil thickens and we cannot reach across the divide between the living and the dead so easily. That's probably where they're getting more power from, the other side. Makes it easier for them to come after us." She reached out to the plate on the table. "I'm going to need another brownie to process all this."

"Me too," Molly said.

"We'll have to make sure we tell the facility that you've had your dessert," Belinda said, smiling.

Molly shuddered. "That woman is a pain in my—"

"Why did you move there?" Nyx interrupted. "I appreciate the house, and I love being here, but we could both live here. There's plenty of room."

Molly's lips thinned. "I didn't want to, but the truth is that if I were here, he wouldn't come after you. I wanted to be alive when this happened, so I could help you."

Nyx's eyes filled with tears. "No—"

"Don't get all teary on me," Molly said. "I'm just being practical. If I weren't here, your mother wouldn't be much help, would she?"

"She's not wrong," Belinda added. "We'd be screwed if we had to depend on your mother. No offense."

Nyx acknowledged this with a short nod. "None taken. Okay, Grandma, tell me exactly how you defeated him."

"I swung a flaming torch at him and burned him. Then he went away."

Nyx and Belinda were silent for a moment. "Well… that shouldn't be too hard," Belinda said. "We just need to make sure you always have a flaming torch with you everywhere you go."

Nyx dropped her head onto the table. "Grandma! How the hell am I supposed to do that?"

Her grandmother shrugged. "I have no idea. I got lucky."

The plan was to lure Kush out of wherever shapeshifters hid so she could be done with all this. The idea of the otherworldly beast waiting to hunt her down was, to put it mildly, unsettling. Better to finish this… whatever it was so she could move on with her life. But as far as plans went, it was shaky at best. Belinda and Molly would position themselves at the 7-11 down the street, parked in the lot and occasionally going inside for candy and drinks (the last part being Molly's idea). Nyx would sit in her backyard at night, torch at her side, ready to be lit. The idea was that if she offered herself up as bait, he would come.

She had slicked her short hair down and left all her jewelry inside. She wore leggings and a fitted flannel pullover because she didn't want him to have anything to grab onto. She stretched out on the lounge chair in the backyard, feeling underneath again to make sure the torch was under her chair. *I'll need to time it when I light it.* She'd practiced inside the house, swinging her legs over the side, reaching under the chair, and pulling the torch and long lighter out. *Piece of cake*, she thought. *I've totally got this. Probably.*

Whatever. She wasn't going to think about it. Maybe, since Halloween was in two days, he would skip her this year.

Siggy sat next to her, for some reason refusing to lie down. She started to pet him, soothed by the dog's presence. "You're my best buddy, aren't you?" she whispered to the dog. He licked her hand.

Siggy growled, low at first then louder. Nyx shivered. *This is it.* Siggy barked once, nose pointing at the gate. A shadowy figure entered, long strides bringing him toward her.

Nyx reached under the chair and pulled out the makeshift torch. She didn't have much time. They had tied a gasoline-soaked rag to a long stick, and when she lit it, the flame caught easily on the rag.

"Nyyyyxxxx…" he sing-songed, otter-like features reflected in the glow of the flame. "Kush is here for our date."

She bent her knees, dropping her center of gravity and ready to defend herself. She held the torch in front of her.

"For me?" he mocked, eyes shining red and face a mask of vicious glee. "Why, thank you!" He stepped forward and grabbed her torch at the middle, forcing it upward and away from his face. While she struggled to yank the torch away from him, he pulled a water bottle from an inside jacket pocket. The wide-mouth Yeti bottle had no cap, and when he reached up and dumped the contents on the torch, the flame sizzled then extinguished.

Insects sang a night song and the scent of smoke permeated the air. Nyx's mind was blank. So much for a plan.

"Your grandmother already did that to me." He stepped closer, still holding onto the torch. "She didn't kill me, obviously, because I left. Fire is definitely one of the things that can do it, though."

Centuries of my family defending themselves and it ends with me, she thought. *But I'm not going down without a fight.* She brought her knee up while pushing the torch to her left, trying to catch him off balance. When he moved slightly, she let go of the torch and swung her elbow straight up, trying to catch him on the chin.

He grabbed her arm before she could connect. "Tsk, tsk, Nyx. That's not very nice, now, is it? I'm just here for a friendly little visit."

She grunted and pulled her arm back. "Nobody actually says tsk tsk except losers."

He smiled, his small, pointed teeth white in the moonlight. "You are a delight. I will enjoy consuming your soul. It will be appropriate payback for your family after all the years you have been a hindrance to us."

Shapeshifters had issues, she thought. "I have no idea what you're talking about. I didn't even know of your existence until you talked to me at the gym."

"And you call yourself a guardian?" he sneered.

"No, I don't call myself anything," she said. "What are you talking about?"

He grabbed her chin, forcing her head backward so she looked up at him. "Your family is always saving people from us. Always getting in the way. We survive by consuming souls, and yet you have stopped us time and time again. Because of you, we have gone hungry. Because of you, my family has dwindled. Because of you, we have had to change our ways." He leaned closer. "No more. Tonight, you die. And with that, there will be no more of your family who can stand in our way."

"I don't like you." She swung at him, trying to catch him in the face, but he easily blocked her, lifted her, and threw her to the ground.

He came at her quickly, not even giving her time to raise her legs and kick or fight.

WOOF!

Siggy leaped, landing on Kush, and in an instant had him by the throat. By the time Nyx could sit up, Siggy had dropped him to the ground, nothing more than an otter. A dead otter.

She took a breath, shaking, as Siggy sniffed her face. "I'm okay, boy. Thank you." She wrapped her arms around her dog, burying her face in his fur.

Nyx stood, trying to stop shaking but also not wanting to be on the ground near the dead otter thing. Because… eewww. She pulled her phone out of her pocket and texted Belinda.

Done. It's over.

Five minutes later, Belinda and Molly burst into the backyard. By that time Nyx had turned on the lights, keeping an eye on the dead animal while she did so. Siggy sat in the same spot, apparently watching the otter too.

Her grandmother stopped short, staring at what used to be Kush. "Huh. Nice work."

Belinda hugged her. "Are you okay? Did he hurt you? Did you burn him?"

"Thanks," Nyx said. "I'm fine. No, our plan didn't quite work out the way we wanted, but Siggy saved me." She turned to Molly. "Is this it? Is it over? He said you hadn't killed him with the fire, but right now he looks pretty dead to me. Are there more?"

Molly nodded. "Yes, there are more. And no, it's not over. But at least this part is, which means we can begin the next part of the plan and I can move home and out of that godawful place."

Nyx put her arm around her grandmother. "It will be good to have you here. But you have some explaining to do."

Molly stepped away from Nyx and headed inside. "How about we order a pizza? I'm hungry."

"Grandma, why did he say we are guardians? What are we guarding?"

Molly didn't stop. "Pepperoni sound good? I'll call in the order."

Belinda laughed. "You're not going to get a straight answer out of her until she's ready."

"I know," Nyx said, shaking her head. "But she better start talking soon, because I think more of these… beings are going to start coming for us. Or we have to save others from them. I'm not sure what we're supposed to do." Siggy leaned against her, solid and true.

"Whatever happens, I'm here for all of you," Belinda said.

"All of us?"

"Yeah. You, Molly, and Siggy." She smiled, leaning over and ruffling the dog's fur. "By the way, my mother told me something interesting yesterday." She looked up at Nyx. "Turns out we're more than friends."

Nyx stared at her. "What? What are you talking about?"

Belinda straightened. "My mother's been into genealogy lately. She's traced our family tree all the way back to the dinosaurs or something. Anyway, looks like you and I are distant cousins. We're family."

"That's why you're here," Molly said from the doorway. "Now come inside. The pizza is on the way. We can bury that thing later. For now, we have plans to make."

Author's note: The legend of the Kushtaka, the shapeshifting otter, is from the Tlingit peoples of the Pacific Northwest Coast of North America. There are differing accounts of these creatures, and in some stories they are cruel while in others they are helpful. Stories also relate that the Kushtaka can be kept away through copper, urine, dogs or fire.

About the Author

Narielle Living is the president and founder of Blue Fortune Enterprises, a publishing company that believes that books have the power to change lives. She is also the managing editor for the Williamsburg, Virginia magazine *Next Door Neighbors* and has written hundreds of do-it-yourself articles for online magazines. She is the author of the mysteries *Signs of the South, Revenge of the Past, Christmas in Virginia, Madness in Brewster Square,* and *Birding in Brewster Square,* and she co-authored *Chesapeake Bay Karma—The Amulet.* In addition, her fiction appears in the Chesapeake Bay Writers' anthologies *Christmas on the Bay* and *Harboring Secrets.* She edits both fiction and nonfiction and loves helping other writers achieve their goals.

Narielle is currently working on her next books, which include a mystery in the Brewster Square series and a memoir about adoption.

A Halloween Heed

allison keli

Commander Shepard Boulevard connected NASA Langley Research Center in Hampton, Virginia, to the city of Yorktown. It would grow eerily quiet after the workday unless an event was happening across the street at the Langley Speedway. During late autumn months when the Speedway was closed for the season, the highway became even more silent as the speedway would suddenly be stuck in suspended animation of frozen engine roars emanating from a lonely landscape. At seven p.m. on these nights, the stoplights remained green.

Government fencing covered in barbed wire protected the base from those who didn't belong. Guarded entrances required proper identification to enter the area. At the start and end of the workday, the entrance was besieged with cars awaiting their turn to enter or exit.

A giant, bright blue globe with its emblazoned NASA logo was perched outside of the entrance, offering possibility to everyday passersby. Referred to as the *Meatball*, it typically was the only thing that stood out during the busy hours of onslaught traffic.

This particular evening, this crisp at-dusk Halloween where children were in their neighborhoods in garish and grotesque costumes—or dainty and delicate as it were—parents had torn out of the base, rushing home earlier than normal. While steam blasted from tall stacks on top of buildings peppering the barren terrain, various-sized wind tunnels were still for the day.

The Meatball sat isolated in the chilly breeze.

The few drivers who remained were last ditch attempting to reach their destinations for candy and treats. They were not paying attention to anything other than the green lights propelling them forward.

A flickering, a glimmer, a shimmer, a crackle like ethereal lightning. A rip in the ether occurred alongside the globe. The tear slowly ripped further, creating a slightly visible electromagnetic wave that lost its luster in the new darkness. A slight smell of ionization permeated the air as if billions of Himalayan salt lamps had suddenly been switched to the on position.

The globe was lit up, but next to it, the tear was

completely shrouded in shadow. Even the guards at the gate didn't look up from their cell phones to notice the anomaly.

The tear unhurriedly reached the ground, taking its time, reaching a total of about twenty feet in length. With a shockingly bright flash of light mimicking Heaven's glow, a pulsating vibrance sucked in the Meatball along with a beat-up Honda and its driver who was leaving Langley. The car had just about merged onto the highway, mere seconds away from a normal drive home.

The other drivers on the road didn't see; the people on the base didn't know.

Transformer sounds aloft, the tear rapidly glued itself upwards in a zipper fashion, sealing the fate of the car and the *blue* Meatball inside of it.

Now in its place was a red-orange globe, gently blinking in the darkness alongside the distant stars in the sky. The logo no longer read NASA; it now read MARSx. Tiny little jack-o'-lanterns sat just beneath the behemoth globe, dotting the perimeter of the globe where they once had not been.

The small handful of cars driving on the boulevard paid no mind to the globe they saw every day during their evening commute. The guards never noticed a difference, either.

So quickly reality changed. So little notice given to the paradigm shift.

allison keli loves Halloween so much, she actually got married on October 31st… in Salem, Massachusetts… during a blue moon… by a green witch… at Ropes Mansion, aka Allison's house from *Hocus Pocus*!

allison is a STEM educator, bodyworker and workshopper. Her varied interests have led her to write on numerous topics. As a massage therapist, she writes about holistic health and spiritual themes at www.SwellnessVibes.com. As a mom, she writes about parenting at www.FlightoftheSeedling.Wordpress.com.

Her books include a children's fantasy/science mash-up about the Perseid Meteor Shower. In *Phenix & Fox: Shooting Stars*, her young son helped create some of the illustrations. Her adult magical realism series, *The Light Thrower*, currently contains two full-length novels: *When Violet Got Bored* and *When Violet Took Flight*. Full of humor and kitschy pop culture references, the novels tackle hard questions about destiny and free will.

allison's semi-historical spookfests, *The Hauntings of DoG Street*, started as a series on the now defunct Kindle Vella. The third novella in the series, *The Wren Building*, will be published in the fall of 2025. The first two novellas, *Chowning's Tavern* and *Bruton Parish Church*, introduce us to a college student who discovers she has a knack for speaking with 18th century ghosts who still have stories to tell.

allison lives in SE Virginia with her two kitties, rising middle schooler son, and firefighting husband. Visit her at www.allisonkeli.com for more fun and mayhem!

Tip-Tap

Sonja McGiboney

As the weak light of sunrise shone through the cellar window, I could finally see the faces of the creatures that had tip-tapped through my dreams. They weren't dreams.

I was on my belly, my cheek on the cold concrete. I tried to move but pain shot through my body. I laid my head back down, not sure if the pain I felt was worse than admitting that Sue was right.

Before our separation, she told me there were mice down here and asked me to get rid of them. I never did because I never saw any. Neither did I take care of the dampness that made the entire basement section of this eighteenth-century house smell like sewage and armpits.

We didn't always argue. In fact, at one time our love was strong, even when our families didn't want us to marry. Though both from Virginia, she was raised in a mansion in Williamsburg while I spent my youth surviving in the Newport News projects. But I made something of myself. I sold cars for a living and was good at it. I worked my way up to manager and soon took over the place. I made thousands from commissions.

I wanted to do the right thing and make her parents proud. But when I asked her father if I could marry her, he said no.

Can you imagine… I'd brought myself out of the poorest of situations and could afford two of their mansions, but I wasn't good enough for his daughter.

So, we eloped. It just so happened that the appointment to see the judge was on October thirty-first. We asked our best friends to be witnesses. They teased us about the date. "It ain't good to be getting hitched on the same day that the saints and sinners are running around."

Sue looked me in the eye when she heard that and said, "It doesn't matter what kind of ghosts and goblins are running around. They won't ever come between us. Nothing will."

Our first few years of marriage were terrific. Her parents tolerated me. We found a historic home with some land north of Williamsburg. Her mom warned us that we'd go nuts being by ourselves, so far from the city, but we loved it.

Our goals for the house and our lives, which were so

similar in the beginning, soon changed. She wanted to build a porch on the back, and I thought the place didn't need one. She wanted me to go on double dates with her new friends, I wanted to stay home and watch the games or go to the games with my buddies.

And then there were the mice. Every time I tried to do something, nothing happened. They didn't fall into any of the traps. I even tried some of those homemade ones with a wire crossing over a deep bucket. But there were never any mice to catch. That's when I realized that she might be going a little crazy and was seeing things that weren't there.

I didn't have time to look for mice. My car business was booming. I bought several other dealerships in other states, which took me out of town a lot.

Sue became clingy. She didn't want me leaving anymore. I started working late just to avoid going home. Alone more than not, Sue started involving herself in committees and clubs. Then the baby thing. She couldn't seem to get pregnant. She blamed me. If I were home more, if I took her traveling with me, things would be better. On and on and on she whined. By the time I decided to leave, we were living like roommates.

I don't remember why she did it, but I came home after a two-week trip and she had dug up all the floorboards. She was sitting on the floor, dirt in her hair, holding a metal box.

"Sue, what happened?" Her eyes were glassy and she looked possessed.

When she spoke, her voice was thin, like she was talking through a tin can. "The mice. Honey, you need to get rid of the mice. They're all over the place. Don't you see them?"

I never saw them. She was never quite right after that. A few months later, after one of the loudest, most horrific arguments we ever had that involved throwing lamps and breaking dishes, I decided I needed to leave before she killed me.

Now here I was, I think in our cellar. Last thing I remembered, we were eating dinner. Sue had called me on the day before our anniversary to say she wanted to talk. We'd been separated for three years and I thought we'd be discussing the settlement.

I noted the fancy table setting when I came in and, even though the meal wasn't fancy, that didn't fire off any warnings in my brain. Sue always liked fancy things. We spent time talking about the good ole' days. She even brought up the mice, saying she still saw them.

She hadn't yet brought up the subject of divorce when she asked me to get more beer from the cellar. I don't remember anything clearly after that. My head filled with vague images. Ones of her holding my arm as we walked down the rickety wooden steps intertwined with the sound of her laughter at the dinner table as she pushed me to drink some more. Before passing out, I remember wondering, "Did she drug me?"

I lifted my eyes and watched the mice run back and forth in front of me. There must have been at least a hundred of them running around. Creepy how they walked all over my arms and legs like I was a plush carpet.

I shook my head. Why was I down here? I got to get out of here. I tried to move, but ropes on my ankles and wrists held me. "What is going on?"

When I tried to roll over, pain shot through my body. I couldn't move. In the effort, the cold concrete rubbed my cheek raw, and I could smell the mouse droppings that were inches from my face. The gurgle in my stomach warned me. I swallowed but it kept coming. I arched my back to raise my head off the floor but it wasn't enough to keep at bay the expulsion of beer, garlic, and pizza.

When the retching ended and I smelled like a pig in a stable, I realized that I had no idea how I'd gotten into this predicament.

A few mice started eating my vomit, and I dry heaved.

I opened my eyes after passing out and had to blink a few times from the bright light. When my eyes adjusted, I saw twenty or so mice enjoying the retched feast. They were so cute and they reminded me of a few pets I had growing up. Sue hated them and said that the smelly varmints always creeped her out.

One mouse, a brown one with white markings,

looked up and stared into my eyes. It approached slowly as if it were shopping and deciding if it wanted to buy something. Its whiskers wiggled as its nose twitched.

Groggily, I looked at it. My voice croaked when I spoke. "Hey, you're a cute-looking mouse."

My brain cleared instantly when the cute mouse bit my lip and held on. "Ouch! You stupid mouse!" I ignored the pain and shook off the mouse. It scampered back to its friends. They all turned to look back at me.

I wiggled around, trying to turn onto my back. I had to get up off the floor. Pain started at my toes, shot up my body, and exploded in my head. Desperately, I forged ahead.

After three tries and excruciating pain, I managed to flip over onto my back. Though my hands were still tied behind my back, I used them as leverage, like the third leg of a tripod, to push myself up. The effort made my head swim. With pain exploding everywhere, I struggled and finally got into a sitting position.

I closed my eyes until the waves of nausea passed. When I opened them, I saw my twisted leg. My feet were bound at the ankles, but my shin bone formed a perfect V. Shin bones shouldn't have bends in them. Nausea hit me again.

In that moment, I realized that I wouldn't be walking out of the basement without help. "Help! Someone, help! Sue, please, for God's sake, help me!"

Nobody answered, but the few mice that were near me scattered then slowly returned to the pile of vomit. The effort to sit up drained me but the idea of mice eating my face kept me upright.

I tried scooting closer to the wall, but my shoulders had tightened from my hands being tied behind me for so long and wouldn't work. I tried using my good leg to scoot backward. Pain on top of pain hit me. "Aaagh! Damn."

I cried. I cried because of the pain. I cried from the feeling of helplessness. Then I cried because I peed myself.

I heard a noise and woke, realizing that I must have passed out again. The sun no longer lit the room. I was on my side and my cheek rested on the floor again. I stared up at the dark window until my brain finally put together the noise I heard. Footsteps. "Hello? Help me." My voice creaked.

The light came on and two tan boots appeared in front of me. Sue's face came into focus as she knelt down.

"How ya feeling, David?"

"Susan, what's going on?" I tilted my head to see her better.

"It's obvious, isn't it. You're all tied up with nowhere to go."

My eyes grew larger. "What are you doing? Look, I'll do anything you ask, give you anything you want. Just let me go."

"Oh, David, you don't get it, do you? We've been doing just fine these last three years. I loved our arrangement, and I never gave up hope that we'd get back together."

I realized that she must be delusional if she thought we were getting back together. I should have started divorce proceedings earlier, but I was worried she'd freak out and do something irrational. In the past year, she'd seemed sturdier, more put together. "But I thought you had moved on, you know, with Charlie."

"No, David, I was screwing Charlie like you were screwing that whore, Katie."

"Look, if it's the alimony you are worried about losing, I'll put in a clause to keep paying you. I'll give you the house too."

"You know, David, that's not the issue here. You left me. You left me tied up in knots. For over two years, I couldn't function properly. I felt betrayed. I felt alone. I felt broken." With each phrase, spittle flew out of her mouth and hit me in the face. "You threw money my way, but I didn't care about money. You didn't file for divorce, so I thought there was a chance. You've been so nice this last year."

Sue stood, walked out of my view then returned with a box. She set the box in front of my face. "But you had to go and file for a divorce. You really think I'd let you go? After all we've been through?"

I watched with tear-filled eyes as she slowly opened

the box. A flap lifted with each of her next words.

Swish. "You will always be mine."

Swish. "I don't want alimony."

Swish. "I want all of you."

Swish. "Alive or dead."

She reached inside the box and pulled out a commercial-sized jar of peanut butter and a bag of assorted seeds.

I laughed in relief. I thought she'd have a weapon or something in there. Then she pulled out the rubber gloves and she started teasing me. "Sue, I'll do anything. Please don't do this. I won't file for a divorce, I promise. I'll be the husband you always wanted me to be. I'll do anything. Just let me go."

The rubber gloves snapped into place.

I tried wriggling away. The pain paralyzed me.

She opened the jar and pulled out a gob of peanut butter. "I hear you, David. I really do. But none of your other promises ever happened. Why, look at this mouse population. If you'd taken care of it before, it wouldn't be this bad."

"Sue, I beg you. Don't do this."

"I like hearing you beg." Sue slathered my face with peanut butter. "It kind of reminds me of when I begged you not to leave me." Then she affectionately tapped my nose. "Do you remember, honey?"

"I was young. I didn't know what I was doing." I

groaned. "I've learned how to be better. Please don't do this!"

When she slathered my legs, I tried pulling away then screamed in pain. "Aaaahhh!"

She ignored me and used up the rest of the jar on my hair and arms. When she reached for the bag of seeds, I briefly thought of all the pinecone bird feeders we made as kids. Holy cow, she was making me into a feeder for the mice.

I panicked like I've never panicked before. I ignored all the pain and tried to roll over and knock into her. My agonized body betrayed my mind and barely moved.

Her eyes glistened as if she wasn't behind them anymore. I thought back to our wedding night and wondered that maybe she had been touched by a ghost that day. I croaked. "Sue... please?"

She laughed. "Poor David. It sucks to be helpless." She dropped the empty bag of seed and said, "Happy Anniversary, darling. Oh, and happy Halloween." She turned and walked out of my sight. I heard her gentle tip-tap as she walked up the stairs and the soft snap of the basement door as it closed.

I prayed but it didn't do any good. I heard, then felt, the tip-tap of their feet before they sank their teeth into my skin.

Though born in Pennsylvania and recently moved to Alabama, Sonja McGiboney calls herself a Virginian, having lived twenty-seven years between the cities of Newport News, Yorktown, and Smithfield. After graduating from West Virginia University, she married Dale and accompanied him on his twenty-five-year military career. She has two wonderful children, Rachel and Ryan, and grandchildren Theo and Liam.

In writing her books, Sonja pulls from her life experience from moving with Dale and the Army. She has been a piano teacher, substitute teacher, primary teacher, file clerk, gas-station attendant, Family Readiness Group (FRG) Support assistant, FRG leader, mail clerk, credit reference associate, nanny, library assistant, photographer, and author.

In 2015, Sonja and Dale adopted a puppy and named her Jazzy. It was only natural that Sonja, a professional photographer, document Jazzy's antics. Jazzy's first photo album opened a path of creativity which generated 22 more Jazzy books, several non-Jazzy books, and a love of writing beyond children's pictures books.

Sonja's short stories are published in two anthologies, several online flash fiction sites, and her shortest story is published on https://101words.org. She is currently working on several fantasy novels for middle-grade students and a collection of short stories for adults.

You can find Sonja via her website at https://sonjamcgiboney.wixsite.com/sonjamcgiboney

You can find Jazzy's books for ages two through ten at https://www.jazzysbooks.com/

Halloween Is For Monsters

Patti Gaustad Procopi

Timothy remembered the first time he ran something over. He had just gotten his license and was driving with the windows down and the radio blaring. Such pure freedom. Suddenly he spotted something in the road. He didn't have time to swerve, and he ran over it.

The incredible crunchy sound sent electric charges pulsing through him. This was the most amazing thing he had ever experienced. In the rearview mirror, he saw that whatever it was now appeared completely flattened on the road. A turtle, he thought. What else would make such a satisfying crunching sound?

Better than sex, he laughed, even though in truth he had no experience with sex. What girl would look at him?

He couldn't tell his mother about it. She would see

it as some sign of the Devil. In the years since his father had died, his mother had become a religious fanatic. It started with the mega-churches on TV. Then the more she read the Bible, the more she became convinced of the Devil's real presence in the world. Hour after hour she would sit reading Revelations over and over again. When he came home from school, she interrogated him about any satanic encounters he'd had during the day. "Timothy," she intoned, "did you stay pure today? Avoid temptation?"

"I go to high school, Mom. Not much devil worshipping going on there."

All the simple joys of childhood were denied him. No presents from Santa Claus, who his mother deemed a minion of the Devil (Santa = Satan). Easter did not include chocolate eggs from the Easter Bunny. ("Is the Easter Bunny mentioned in the Bible?" his mother roared.) And no dressing up or trick-or-treating on Halloween. In his mother's mind that was Satan's night, and his demons walked the earth. They stayed in the house, with the lights off, and prayed.

One Halloween night when he was about eight, his mother fell asleep and Tim snuck out. He saw lots of children in fancy costumes, laughing as they went up to people's houses and got candy. Tim was upset he hadn't put some kind of costume on. He'd like some candy. Didn't seem much like devil worship to him. Just fun.

A tall figure in a dark robe with a mask obscuring its face suddenly appeared in front of Tim. This was no child. Tim was horrified when he realized the creature wasn't wearing a mask, that its face looked like it had burned and melted. Two tiny lights gleamed where its eyes should be. The figure leaned close to Tim and whispered in a deep voice, "I am the monster your mother warned you about. Why are you here?" Then the figure straightened and laughed. Tim ran home as quickly as he could. He almost slammed the door when he got back home but remembered his mother was asleep, so he shut the door quietly and went up to his room. It took a long time for his heart to stop pounding.

On weekends, his mom went with her Bible and a portable loudspeaker to stand in the middle of Merchant's Square. While everyone enjoyed their day shopping or dining with friends, she would berate them for their sins, warning them of the end of days. Of course he was forced to join her because she couldn't carry the boom box, the loudspeaker, and all her brochures by herself. He would help her set up and then go sit on a bench and pretend he had nothing to do with this woman screaming about the Four Horsemen of the Apocalypse and how there was still time to repent and save your soul.

If he saw people he knew from school, he'd duck his head and pretend he didn't know the woman in the square. But they all knew. Everyone at school teased him about his "crazy" mother. "Tim," they'd said with a laugh, "which Horseman are you today?" No one wanted to be friends with him, the son of a Bible-thumping nut job.

His mother ruined his life. He couldn't wait until he graduated from high school. Then he would take the car and drive off into the sunset. Leave her and the rest of his pathetic life behind.

Reality set in the minute he walked off the stage with his diploma. He had no money. The car belonged to his mother. How was he going to leave? If he took the car, she'd probably call the police and have him arrested. Tell them he was possessed by the Devil and led into sin, which would end up with him starting his adult life in prison.

He got a job as a pizza delivery driver. There was no chance of leaving home or getting a better job. This job did have the advantage of evening work, so he didn't have to spend time with his mother, who always wanted to read Bible passages to him, warning him of the wages of sin. "It's death," she'd shriek. "Repent now."

"Got it Mom. No sin for me," he always said as he walked up to his room. At least he had the excuse that he needed to sleep during the day, so he could avoid almost any interaction with her.

The best part was that the job as a delivery driver gave him the opportunity to run over more turtles. It started with the turtles. He got such a rush hearing that crunching snap when he flattened one on the road. He soon graduated to other creatures. From turtles he moved on to frogs. He loved driving at night after a rainstorm when the roads were full of frogs. Hot, wet summer nights equated to a frog holocaust for him. Snakes were another favorite. He would angle the wheels of the car to run over their middles or their tails, not killing them outright, so he could watch them writhe in agony in the rearview mirror.

One day he actually managed to massacre an entire family of ducklings. They were crossing the road behind their mother when he came upon them. A little clever maneuvering and he nailed all six. In his rearview mirror, he saw the mother duck run back, waddling from one baby to the next. One still flopped around, but the rest were smashed. He imagined her quacking at them and wondering why they didn't get up and follow her.

He loved coming across possums and raccoons. The possums were easy. They were so slow, and it didn't take much to swerve over them. Raccoons were quicker, but he also had good success with them. Squirrels weren't much of a challenge. Almost suicidal, they would throw themselves under the wheels of his car. Once he got two at a time.

His mom stopped going to Merchant's Square on weekends and began complaining of various issues—aches, pains, shortness of breath. He paid no attention to her. "Yeah, Mom, sorry to hear it," told her as he walked up to his room. "Maybe you should pray about it."

He was shocked when he came home and found her dead in her chair with the Bible on the floor in front of her. He kicked the Bible into the corner and called an ambulance. He wanted to kick her as well. The paramedics said it looked like a heart attack and asked if she had heart issues. What could he say? That he had no idea? That he never even spoke to his mother if he could help it? So he said yes. She did. It wasn't like they were going to do an autopsy. Then Tim started making up stuff about her being afraid of doctors even though he begged her to go. He managed to look sad and a bit teary-eyed. The paramedic nodded sympathetically. Tim didn't really know why he wanted the paramedic to feel sorry for him.

He had her cremated. He was taken aback when the funeral parlor called to say he needed to pick up her cremains. What the hell kind of word was that? Why were they always making up new words? Obviously it was two words made into one: cremation and remains. How creepy was that? He didn't want her damn cremains.

When he went by, they handed him a cardboard box with her ashes. What the hell was he supposed to do with that? He took a drive down an old country road and threw the box out the window. "Bye, Mom," he yelled as he rolled the window back up. "May you rot in Hell."

That made him laugh. Wouldn't she be surprised if she ended up in Hell. For what she did to him, Hell was too good for her. He drove on with a big smile on his face.

Tim was shocked when he looked through her papers and found she had managed to save a tidy sum of money. He went to the bank and cleaned out her accounts. Next, he called a realtor and said he wanted to sell his mother's house. Quickly. Too many memories. That got him more sympathy. He wanted away from all the memories. Of her. Of his miserable, lonely childhood. And the smell of her. That smell he had endured for forty years. Sweat, stale clothes, and talcum powder.

He wanted a house out in the country, far from the prying eyes of neighbors who he knew had been spying on him his whole life. No more curtains twitching as they peeked out at him whenever he left the house. Watching him. Laughing at him. Giving him disgusted looks when he saw them in their yards.

He found a little place and moved in immediately. Tim didn't bring one single item from his old house. He wished he could have burned down the house with all the furniture and knick-knacks inside. He wanted no memories of his mother or his past. Then he quit his job. If he was frugal, he could manage. His only real expense was gas. He felt compelled to continue to drive, looking for prey.

On one of his drives, he noticed a young boy and his

dog. They must have lived close by and seemed to spend a good deal of time walking up and down the road. There wasn't apparently much to do out in the country. He began to hate that boy and dog. They seemed so happy and content with each other. Why couldn't he have had a dog? It would have made up for having no friends. His mother wouldn't allow it. She said dogs stank and drooled and peed in the house. Maybe she even said they were the spawn of Satan. Everything was the spawn of the Devil, according to his mother. He laughed bitterly. Didn't matter now. He'd rather be alone.

One evening driving back home, he saw the dog walking along the road by itself. He wondered briefly where the boy was before swerving and hitting the dog. It had been an automatic response to an animal in the road. Right before the impact, the dog turned and looked at him with an almost human expression of shock before it went flying through the air. It landed in a ditch, and he continued home. It had been his biggest target yet. He felt quite pleased.

The next day when he drove out, he saw the boy, his face stained with tears, walking up and down the road calling for his dog. The boy flagged him down and asked if he had seen his dog. "No," he said. "Not recently." The boy stifled a sob and nodded his thanks. He drove on. He experienced an odd twinge of guilt, but he suppressed it. The boy shouldn't have let the dog wander out on its own.

The following day, he saw the boy and some adults standing around near where he had hit the dog. They were lifting something out of the ditch and putting it in the back of a truck.

A month later, he was shocked to see the boy and the dog again walking along the road. The dog appeared to be limping badly, though overwise it appeared fine. The boy had a huge grin on his face. As he drove by, the dog turned and gave him a look of pure hatred. It almost scared him.

Halloween was coming up. How he had wanted to dress up and go trick-or-treating with the other kids when he was little. The one time he'd tried he ran into that creepy character. Tim laughed. Just some teenager fooling around, scaring kids. Now he would get his revenge on all those happy children. It would serve the little creeps right. Going around dressed in costumes, begging for candy. He could almost hear his mother screaming, "Devil worshippers," when she saw the kids going door to door.

Tim had decided he was going to try for his biggest prize yet. A child or maybe two. He would have to be very careful and make sure no one saw him. If he went to another neighborhood, he'd be able to swoop through before anyone noticed him. He was nervous. This was big. He wondered if a child would fly up in the air like the dog had. Maybe bounce off the hood of the car. That would be exciting, though he hoped they wouldn't go through the windshield.

Halloween night finally arrived. It occurred to him that he hadn't actually been out on Halloween night since the time he snuck out when he was eight. No reason to go out and just like his mother, he kept the house dark so no one would knock, asking for candy.

He prepped the car by covering the license plates with mud. That way no one could see his plate number. His car was pretty nondescript. He imagined the police asking witnesses what color or make the car was and they would mumble, "Black… or navy… just some kind of sedan. An ordinary car."

Putting a knit cap on his head, he darkened his face. Tim looked in the mirror and laughed. He was finally going to go out dressed up for Halloween. "Hey kids, I'm a monster. They really do exist and you'll find that out tonight. Tonight you will get a trick instead of a treat."

He drove about five miles to another neighborhood. Not that anyone knew him but here he was even less known. As he drove along planning his attack, his car coasted to a stop. It hadn't made a sound. Just stopped running. No matter what Tim did, he couldn't get any response from the engine. He was angry that his evening plans were going sideways. Stepping out of the car, he opened the hood and looked in. He knew nothing about engines, so he shut the hood again and considered his situation. He saw houses ahead and children running across the street, laughing. It would have been perfect.

He began walking, heading to the closest house. Maybe he'd joke and say trick or treat to explain the makeup on his face. They'd laugh and then let him make a phone call or maybe even drive him home. Tim hadn't gone far when he heard a car coming up behind him. He turned to face the car, happily thinking he might flag it down and get a ride.

The car slowed down. Tires squealing, it suddenly sped up and swerved toward him. Stunned, he reacted slowly. Before he could leap out of the way, the front end of the car caught him and flung him head over heels into the bushes next to the road.

Amazingly, he never lost consciousness. The sensation of flying was actually fun but then he landed hard and rolled down into a ditch. The image of the car swerving and hitting him was hard to comprehend. It was obviously deliberate. Who deliberately runs someone over? he wondered and then laughed bitterly. The trick had been on him. Maybe there were others out there just like him.

He assessed his situation. He was in a deep ditch with bushes overhead. No one would see him from the road. He tried to move. First his toes. He couldn't feel them. Next his fingers. Nothing. He must be paralyzed, he thought. Hopefully it was only temporary.

Children and parents walked by on the street. Tim

heard them talking and laughing about all the candy they had gotten. Which houses gave out the best. No one noticed him. He tried to call out, but the only sound he made was a strangled moan.

He must have passed out at some point. When he woke with a jolt, it was completely black. Not even a star was out. Everyone had gone home and they were safe and sound asleep in their beds. What did they always say about that time of night? It was the witching hour? This was when the demons roamed, according to his mom.

Tomorrow morning, someone would notice his car and then find him in the ditch. He heard rustling in the brush. What kind of creatures were out there in the dark? Thinking about all the animals he had killed, he hoped they weren't out for revenge.

He lost track of time. Who had been in that car? Why had they hit him and driven off? Obviously, they had done it on purpose. But why?

Karma. That word came out of the deep recesses of his mind. People talked about karma as some kind of force that paid people back for the good and bad things they had done. Was this karma?

The cloying scent of talcum powder filled the air, gagging him. He opened his eyes. His mother leaned over him. "Mom," he croaked. "Help me."

"I can't, son. You did this to yourself. I tried to raise you right. I warned you about the Devil, but you went to the dark side. I tried to save you but you are the spawn of Satan…"

"Mom… please…" his brain screamed. He wanted to tell her this was all her fault but she disappeared.

He needed to calm down. His mother was not there. Morning would come soon. Someone would find him. His ears perked up. He heard a strange sound, like a weight being dragged across the gravel road. Not footsteps, he thought, wondering what on earth it could be. He tried to call out again but nothing in his body worked, other than his ears and eyes. No sound emerged from his lips. As hard as he tried, he could not move. The sound drew closer, as if whatever it was knew where he was.

The sounds stopped and he sensed a presence looming over him. He strained his eyes but couldn't see anything.

"Damn. I can't believe you're still alive," a voice said. "But you must be. I see your eyes darting back and forth."

Tim's blood went cold. He knew this voice. He had heard it once before on that Halloween night when he'd slipped outside his house. Straining his eyes wide, a dark figurine with a face that appeared to be burned black hovered over him.

"Ack…" he gurgled.

Warm breath washed over his cheek. "Ha. Still quite the conversationalist. I thought you'd break your neck when you flipped over into the ditch."

What is happening? he thought. "It seems like you

are completely paralyzed. Can't move. Can't talk." A soft laugh floated over him. "Rather fitting, don't you think?"

"Arrghh…." he moaned.

"I tried to warn you all those years ago. Halloween is when the demons are out. I've actually been waiting for you. I've been watching you all these years. I watched as you did horrible things. But tonight, I had to stop you. I wonder what they'll make of you when they find you. If they find you. You could stay in this ditch for an eternity, slowly decomposing."

This was the creature from that Halloween long ago. Maybe he should have paid more attention to his mother when she said the wages of sin are death. He began to cry. Tears streamed down his face. "Garr…" he tried to scream. He tried to ask for forgiveness. In his head he made all kinds of promises to turn his life around.

"It's late but I think it's still Halloween and you, my friend, have been tricked. Or maybe you've actually finally gotten your just desserts." The deep voice continued. "Shall I leave you to die like you left the dog? Should I drag you out to the street so people can find you? No. I don't want the children to see you. They don't know about your crimes. And you don't deserve a decent burial. After all, you didn't give your mother one."

A hand grabbed Tim's collar and dragged him farther along the side of the road. Then he felt his body rolling down a steep hill and he landed face first in a pool of water.

"Mmm…" he gasped, and bubbles blew in the water.

"They always call for their mother…" The deep voice chuckled from the roadside. "Sadly it's too late. This is my night. You should have stayed home."

The world began to go dark. The last sound Tim heard was a demonic laugh.

About the Author

Patti Gaustad Procopi is a former army brat who lived all over the world before settling in Gloucester, Virginia, with her husband Greg. They raised three daughters and numerous cats and dogs.

Patti worked at two area history museums for thirty-two years. After retiring, she finally had the time to do the thing she always wanted to do: write!

Patti's writing is about emotional connections, friendship and family. Her first novel, *Please…Tell Me More*, was published in 2020 by Blue Fortune Enterprises, LLC, followed by *I'll Get By, Stop Talking,* and *The Murderer You Know*, a podcast mystery.

Patti has had stories printed in literary journals and anthologies and read on a podcast. She's given talks at area libraries and writing symposiums about how to tell your story.

When not writing, Patti enjoys photographing birds on her creek. She also enjoys gardening, yoga, and researching her family genealogy.

You can find Patti's books on Barnes & Noble, Amazon, or wherever books are sold, and you can contact her on her website, pattiproauthor.com, or email patti.pro@cox.net or on Facebook.

Legend Of The Harvest Moon Bringer-Of-Death

Adam Clayton

Scott Newell was normal. Most would say happy. That all changed when he lost his job. *It's due to the economy*, his supervisor said.

Losing his job was devastating. Humiliating. Unfair.

Scott's entire world, his confidence and self-worth, collapsed. Unable to find regular employment, he was reduced to handing out flyers on a street corner and sweeping up parking lots for pennies a day.

Scott could hardly provide for himself, much less his wife and a home. He was soon reduced to bankruptcy, another blow to his self-worth. The final straw was his wife filing for divorce. She'd been the provider; now she was gone.

He was altogether pitiable.

With no means of support, he knew his next stop would be a cardboard box on the street. Scott believed he'd be better off dead.

And then, a breakthrough—of sorts. He was caught trying to steal a loaf of bread from a local bodega. Instead of calling the police, the owner sent him to someone who could help. It turned out to be a job as a file and delivery clerk in a local law firm.

It was a menial and low-paying job, mind-numbingly boring and certainly below him. But he was grateful to have any income, as small as it might be. It allowed him to rent a one-room flat over a garage.

He'd been an English major in college and, as a young man, fancied himself a writer. That dream died long ago, but when a mistaken delivery of books came to the law firm's receiving area, he remembered his youthful passion.

The box was supposed to be filled with dry, boring law review publications. Instead, he found it filled with novels. Mystery novels.

He took the box of novels home and began reading.

The books ignited his imagination, transporting him to new places, and new ways of looking at the world. His passion for writing was reignited. Sitting at his second-hand computer normally used to play games and surf the internet, he began to write a story of his own.

Scott decided to begin with short stories but he

struggled over selecting a genre. He finally settled on urban fantasy. It suited his personal dreams and ambitions.

Pleased with his first story, he believed literary stardom would soon follow. He sent queries to literary agents and magazines, certain a publishing contract would be offered. But it didn't work out that way.

I need a new approach… a new genre that'll really catch readers' attention… something unsettling.

A month later, Scott found a blog: *Imagination Republic.* The blog topics tended to go in wild directions, but as an urban fantasy author, he loved it. This particular blog post focused on urban myths—right up his alley. What piqued his curiosity was the topic: Native American myths and legends.

After reading the *Legend of the Harvest Moon Bringer-of-Death,* he was intrigued. "This might be the answer to jump-starting my literary career," he thought. There wasn't much detail about the myth; it mostly related the hysteria surrounding the appearance of some sort of demon among Native Americans.

He checked online but could find no references, no articles, and no discussions about the story. *How did the blogger get his story?* He searched Blogpros and found the owner of Imagination Republic, a man using the name

ImaJim. After sending a message to ImaJim, he received an email within an hour.

"Great to hear from a subscriber! In answer to your question, *Harvest Moon Bringer-of-Death* is a story I picked up in the Paspahegh Town section of Jamestown Settlement. An older Native American man, working as a historical interpreter, was sitting on a log carving a piece of wood while talking to tourists. When the crowd drifted off, I asked about the Native legends he'd mentioned. That's when he told me the legend…"

At harvest time, when the moon was full, a being would rise from the loamy soil. The smoky form vaguely resembled a man. The beast smelled of rot and sulfur, and a taste hung in the surrounding air like black oil.

They called the spirit-beast Kobaddon.

The beast appeared each year during the harvest and always during the full moon. For three nights, the bringer-of-death was unleashed. Where there was life, death followed— where the spirit passed, mayhem reigned.

Warriors attempting to stop the beast were ripped to pieces, as were any others within sight. Dwellings were smashed and crops mysteriously exploded in flame. Traditional weapons had no effect on Kobaddon.

No one knew how to combat such an enemy. It wasn't flesh-and-blood. It was an evil spirit.

When the bringer-of-death reached the Powhatan settlements, a group of shamans gathered to stop this curse.

The shamans discovered that the demon spirit was unable to cross what was then the Powhatan River, now called the James River.

The spirit went up and down the shore but it could not cross the water. The shamans decided if they could not destroy the evil spirit, perhaps it could be contained.

The shamans waited a full year for the return of the harvest moon and the bringer-of-death. They caught up to Kobaddon outside the Appamatuk settlement.

The shamans surrounded the spirit. Connecting their arms, they called out containment spells. The spirit howled, writhing in agony, and fire shot from its mouth. Unable to break the shamans' spell, there was no escape. Kobaddon was trapped.

The shamans forced the spirit onto a wooden raft and crossed the Appamatuk River, landing on a small islet called Nibi Miskwaw. *In English its name is Sunken Island. During the rainy season only the highest point remains visible above the swollen river waters, thus the name Sunken Island.*

Upon landing, the shamans forced the spirit to the highest point on the island. A pit had been dug and lined with flat stones, each etched with symbols of the containment curse: Eternal imprisonment.

The Kobaddon spirit was cast into the shaft and the pit sealed with a single large stone. From that day Sunken Island was cursed and remained uninhabited.

"That's all I know. Good luck," ImaJim wrote.

Scott had to find Sunken Island and check this story out for himself.

Scott had arranged a few days of vacation and was ready. He had purchased a small tent, a sleeping bag, a folding chair, a camp shovel, a cooler, a battery-powered mini-lantern, a tiny propane stove, MREs for a week, and for show, a fishing rod.

He set out on a clear October day. The drive to Richmond should have taken three hours, but the horrid traffic stretched it to more than four hours. Taking I-295 around Richmond, he exited at US 10 toward Hopewell. As he crossed the Appomattox River, he spotted a small marina.

At the marina office, a weathered, middle-aged man sat at the rental counter. He asked about Scott's plans for the Tracker Bass Boat he was renting. Scott was evasive, mumbling a vague reply about fishing on the Appomattox River.

"Why you wanna go fishin' on this river? Most people use it for fun—you know, water skiing and such."

"I hear the fishing is good," Scott replied.

Shaking his head, the man said, "Don't know where you're gettin' your information, but it's your money…"

With the rental transaction complete, Scott set out.

As the marina disappeared around a bend in the river, he congratulated himself. *I'm glad he didn't ask where I was going. I don't want anyone to know I'm here.*

Sunken Island came into view. Shielding his eyes with the palm of his hand, he saw that the island divided the Appomattox River. Pulling back the throttle, the boat slowed to a crawl and allowed him to search for a landing spot.

The south side of the island was heavily forested, and trees grew at the edge of the water. Moving around the island, he saw the north side was different.

It must be the winds.

For about fifty feet, the bank was clear of trees. Remembering ImaJim's account, he made for the highest area and pulled onto the shore.

He hauled the boat up to the treeline and secured it with a rope. Inspecting his nautical handiwork, he congratulated himself. *Looks good… almost like I know what I'm doing.*

He gazed into the dense foliage. *I wonder if this is the same landing spot the Indians chose hundreds of years before.*

Carrying his supplies made progress slow. Vines hidden under a thick blanket of fallen leaves constantly caught his feet, causing him to stumble and trip. Because thick brush blocked his direct route to the top, he had to detour and retrace his steps. Even though the day was cool, tromping through the underbrush, thick tree growth, and the base of dead leaves was hard, sweaty work.

It's almost like the Island's working against me. I should have brought a machete.

He finally broke through to the high point. From this height, he surveyed the half-mile length of the island. Everywhere he saw forest, yet this area he'd just stepped into was curiously bare. *I wonder why?*

Then he remembered the warning from ImaJim's account:

Sunken Island was cursed.

Compared to the lush foliage everywhere else, this open space does look cursed.

Dropping his load, he walked the perimeter of the open area. *It can't be more than thirty feet in diameter.* He found nothing unusual. There was no sign that any human had ever been in this place.

By the time he'd pitched his tent, rolled out the sleeping bag, and set up the camp stove, the sun was setting.

I'll bet it gets dark out here. Can't really search until sunrise.

After crawling into his tent, he took out his phone and was grateful to have cell service. He watched a movie and then decided he was tired from the drive and the excitement of finding Sunken Island. Sounds of crickets chirping, frogs croaking, and a night breeze rustling the dead leaves in the trees created a soothing rhythm that soon put him to sleep.

Scott woke up with a start. His phone read midnight.

A little confused, he wondered what had awakened him so suddenly. He heard nothing. Absolutely nothing. Not even the rustle of leaves in the trees. The night had gone completely quiet.

Poking his head from the tent, he saw the moon had risen. It looked full, bathing the silent world with a cool luminescence. He shivered and wondered if this silence was normal.

Thump.

Goosebumps raised on his arms and a bolt of fear shot through him.

Where's that sound coming from?

He tilted his head.

Thump.

He spun around, unable to place the source of the sound.

The thump repeated a third time.

It sounds like it's coming from somewhere in the open area.

Ignoring the check he felt in his gut, he went in search of the sound.

Scott moved with deliberate slowness in the moonlight, trying not to make any noise. He walked a few steps, stopped, listened, and then went on.

What the hell could it be?

At the opposite side of the clearing, he put his hands on his hips in frustration. The thumping had stopped.

Nothing.

As he made his way back to the tent, the nighttime sounds returned.

Why did the night sounds stop? If this were a horror movie, I'd say it was because some monster was nearby.

He plopped down on his sleeping bag but was unable to get back to sleep.

The next morning, Scott was up early. In the light of day, he felt ridiculous about his unreasoning fear. *I'm letting that legend get to me.* He made coffee and planned out his search for the purported burial pit of the Harvest Moon Bringer-of-Death.

Scott's search was methodical. He began searching the perimeter of the roughly circular clearing and worked his way toward the center. The morning passed and by the afternoon, he had found nothing of interest.

Standing in the center of the clearing, he looked around and said, "Maybe it's all just a myth—the kind of thing adults tell their children to make them behave."

Returning to the campsite, he selected a pouch of freeze-dried beef stew and boiled it as directed. He reviewed ImaJim's story again, hoping to find clues to the pit's location.

He walked the center of the clearing and again found nothing. Then it occurred to him. *It's been what—four hundred years? I could be standing right on the pit and not know it.*

A thrill shot through him, realizing that had to be right. He ran back to the camp, picked up the shovel, and returned to the center of the clearing.

If I were going to dig a hole to contain the supposed spirit, I'd put it in the middle of this clearing.

He began digging but found the ground strangely resistant to his little camp shovel.

There must be clay in this soil.

Digging took longer than expected. Wiping his brow, Scott noticed the setting sun.

It looks like there could be something buried here. A little more digging, and it should be visible.

Twenty more minutes of digging and still nothing. Then, as he was about to give up for the day, his shovel tip struck something hard. He tapped around, testing its size. With renewed attention, Scott dug around the obstruction. Standing back in his three-foot hole, he let out a soft whistle.

"It's really here."

Scraping more soil off the stone, its shape became clear: It was square, each side measuring about twenty-four inches. The stone had etched carvings and faded paintings depicting animals of prey—wolf, mountain lion, and eagle. All the images were in positions of attack.

Scott worked the triangular tip of his shovel under one side of the stone and tried unsuccessfully to lever it up. He climbed out of the pit to catch his breath and think.

It's sealed in this clay soil. I'm going to need a longer lever... and a fulcrum.

He toyed with continuing his exploration by moonlight but gave it up and returned to camp.

The next morning, he awoke refreshed. There'd been no interruption of his sleep, and coupled with his discovery of what surely must be the burial pit capstone, he was energized. After a quick breakfast of a protein bar and a cup of camp coffee, he went into the forest in search of a lever.

Plenty of trees surrounded the clearing. Most still had dead leaves clinging, but that wasn't what he was looking for. He went in search of a suitable piece of deadwood.

Scott found a large tree that had fallen and selected a sturdy-looking branch. Prying it back-and-forth, it finally separated from the trunk and he held it up for inspection.

This should do nicely.

At the tent, he retrieved a folding knife. The three-inch blade was wide and stout, well-suited for trimming and shaping. After cutting off the smaller shoots, he considered the branch end.

This won't fit under that capstone.

Setting the branch across his lap, he began slicing and shaping. An hour of work resulted in a reasonably good lever. Returning to the pit, he picked up a large rock.

Here's my fulcrum.

Standing over the pit, he realized the cleared space wasn't enough to fit his lever.

I need to dig this out a little more.

It didn't take long to clear an additional two feet from the capstone, but it was getting dark.

I guess this'll wait until tomorrow.

Back at the camp, Scott prepared a meal. Sitting in his camp chair and balancing the plate on his knees, he watched the moonrise.

It's a full moon. What did that old Indian say about that?

He found ImaJim's message on his phone and read the account again, this time focusing on the full moon reference.

The spirit beast appeared each year during the harvest, always during the full moon. For three nights the bringer-of-death was unleashed. Where there was life, death followed—where the spirit passed, mayhem reigned.

A swift breeze blew across the clearing. Dead leaves rustled and tree branches creaked. The crickets stopped chirping and the frogs stopped croaking. The wind was cold and it passed right through him, chilling him to the bone.

It's damn spooky out here.

With that, he retreated to the imagined safety of the tent.

After eating a quick breakfast, Scott returned to the pit with the trimmed branch. Reaching the edge, he felt a shudder under his feet.

What was that?

Fear gripped him and he waited.

Will it happen again?

Nothing. He let out the breath he'd been holding.

I've got myself spooked… I've taken that story too seriously.

He dropped into the pit and set the tip of the branch under the capstone. Before he could begin, there was a deep *thump* from beneath the stone.

His knuckles went white as he gripped the branch lever, and beads of sweat dripped down his forehead. His heart began racing.

Thump.

This time the capstone jumped slightly before dropping back into place. His stomach tightened.

Scott dropped the branch and bolted from the pit.

Once inside the tent, he huddled in the rear corner, holding his knees to his chest.

Scott sat the entire night in that huddled position, unable to sleep. It gave him time to think about what he'd experienced.

The more he thought about it, the more he convinced himself that there was nothing to fear.

You're a damn fool, Scott Newel. It's probably just the Appomattox running below this island. Yeah, that's it—the river. Gotta be what's making that sound, and when I pried up that stone, it must have released pressure.

Scott decided to face his fear but not until sunrise.

By six in the morning, the sky had lightened. Crawling to the tent flap, he felt a little foolish.

Was I really thinking that zipping up a nylon flap would keep some unearthly thing from getting in?

He opened the tent flap and poked his head out. Fog filled the clearing. He couldn't see ten feet in front of him. Scott shivered.

I'll wait a while. Let the fog burn off.

By seven o'clock, the fog had given way to a heavy overcast sky.

I can't sit in here all day.

After a quick breakfast, he felt normal and chided himself for reacting so foolishly the night before.

I even left all my equipment in the pit.

He returned to the center of the clearing and

inspected his little dig. Everything was down there: the branch, the stone fulcrum, and the shovel. Despite his newfound bravado, Scott was hesitant to jump back into the pit. He first circled it, inspecting the capstone from all angles. After satisfying himself there was no danger, he jumped in.

Scott dug the pointed end of the branch under the stone cover while bracing it on the fulcrum stone. With a heave, he pried up the capstone. A small twist rotated the stone enough to leave the pit partially open. He sat and used his legs to push the capstone fully off the pit opening.

On all fours, he crept to the edge and looked in. It smelled terrible. He almost gagged at the intense miasma—like a decomposed animal mixed with rotten eggs, leaving something like a motor oil taste on his tongue.

There was only darkness below. Turning his head to one side, he listened.

Silence.

Taking his Maglite, he shined the beam into the pit and saw clay tablets set into the circular walls. He remembered ImaJim's account.

A pit had been dug and lined with flat stones etched with symbols of the containment curse.

The flashlight showed just enough to verify they were etched symbols. Some were painted figures, like those on the capstone.

The Kobaddon spirit was cast into the shaft and the pit was sealed with a single large stone.

It seems I've found the pit of the legend, but where is this Kobaddon spirit?

He'd neglected to bring a rope or other climbing gear—another amateur oversight. In this oddly dark shaft, he couldn't see much, even with the flashlight. He grabbed a nearby stone and dropped it. Scott expected to hear a splash that would confirm the river did run below the island, but there was nothing. Not even the sound of the stone striking the bottom.

How deep did those native warriors dig?

He fussed around the pit for a long time, taking pictures with his phone, cleaning off the capstone, and wondering how all this might work in the story he hoped to write.

The thought of a new story was exciting. Sitting on the edge of his pit, legs dangling, he daydreamed through the afternoon.

Scott returned to his campsite to think about his next moves. The sun was setting, casting a warm glow over the clearing. He thought it quite peaceful. As he stowed his gear in the tent, he noticed the fishing pole. It gave him an idea.

I don't have a rope but I do have a fishing pole, and it's still light enough to drop a line. At least I'll know how deep it is.

With fishing pole in hand, he walked back to the pit. An icy breeze came up, rustling the dead leaves.

I can't let that spook me. This isn't Sleepy Hollow, it's just wind in the trees.

It was almost sundown, but he judged there was still time to test the pit's depth.

If I find anything, I'll come back in the morning.

Sitting on the capstone, he dropped the line into the pit. The reel spun only a moment before stopping. *Not as deep as I thought—maybe eight or ten feet.*

Then he felt a slight tug, like a fish nosing the hook. *Maybe there's water down there after all.*

It tugged again, this time with more force. Scott began to reel his line in but after a few turns, the line went taut.

Pulling the pole tip up gently two or three times, he hoped to set the hook in whatever he'd caught.

The line went tighter, pulling the pole tip down sharply. He yanked up on the pole.

Must be a big fish.

Holding onto the pole with both hands, he stood to gain better leverage. Then he heard a deep growl, like some kind of primeval beast. True fear gripped him.

A sudden downward pull caused Scott to lose his balance. Still holding onto the pole, he fell into the open pit. Too late, he let go.

He fell heavily, landing on a surprisingly spring-like surface. Winded for a moment, he tried inhaling but gagged and almost passed out.

I must have fallen on… what?

Overwhelmed by the stench, he lay there almost paralyzed. *Whatever I've fallen on, I don't want to disturb it.*

Something gripped him by the shoulders and in the murky, fog-like mist, two bright red orbs appeared.

Eyes!

Enveloped, he was unable to move. He was trapped.

The menacing, primeval growl filled the air as his body experienced stabbing pains, as if he were being clawed. He cried out and began to shake uncontrollably with fear.

Then, it all stopped.

Scott was lifted up, like a priest raising a host in offering before being tossed onto the hard earth of the pit.

There was a terrible, loud screech. It was so painful, he had to cover his ears. A smoke-form rose toward the opening above.

Scott sensed he was being left alive. *Why?*

Then he remembered something from the legend, something that made his blood run cold.

…flat stones etched with symbols of the containment curse: eternal imprisonment unless there was a substitute.

With a groan of despair, he realized he was the substitute. *How can I escape?*

Standing and extending his hand upward, he could almost reach the edge of the pit. Almost.

I need something to carve a step into the wall.

The only thing at hand was the fishing pole—certainly not adequate for the job. Panic became terror as the capstone slid over the opening.

"No!" Scott shouted. "Stop! In the name of God, please!"

Scott's cry of horror and despair went unheard. He was trapped in the pit, plunged into a Stygian darkness that only amplified his terror. Sinking to the ground, he pulled his legs up and dropped his face onto his knees.

How long had his sobbing lasted? In this black pit, it was impossible to know. After regaining some measure of self-control, he understood. Despite the Native's warnings, he'd foolishly opened the pit and released the spirit.

I'm trapped just like Kobaddon, the bringer-of-death. I've been left in the demon's place!

He had no delusions of rescue—not now. No one knew he was on the island.

He shut his eyes to block out the darkness, overcome with despair. *What have I done?*

He let out a loud cry.

"What have I let loose on the world?"

Scott prayed for a quick death.

The Harvest Moon Bringer-of-Death, the demon spirit Kobaddon, rose from its pit of confinement. The demon spirit's appearance was like a column of black smoke, but once released, it coalesced into the form of a man.

Its first act was to close the pit. Kobaddon knew well the spells on the pit walls. This substitution was the only escape.

"Let the stupid human take my place," Kobaddon gloated.

The spirit glided across the clearing into the forest beyond, looking for other humans to torment. But the island was uninhabited. With a thundering shout of anger, the spirit Kobaddon would not be denied. It had many years to make up for.

Kobaddon moved swiftly, a path of destruction left behind. Underbrush was set afire, trees cracked and toppled, and dead leaves billowed up like a cloud.

At the flat area along the shore, Kobaddon remembered this part of the island. It took only a moment to find the man's boat tied to a tree. With a low, mirthless laugh, he knew his liberation was at hand.

The smoky form filled the small craft and began crossing the short distance to the mainland.

"Death… destruction… fear. I will not be stopped again!"

About the Author

Adam Clayton has been writing novels for twenty years. Before that, he owned and operated a Los Angeles-based production company providing a wide range of creative services including: script writing, speech writing, film writing, multi-media and live event production.

Adam developed domestic and international marketing campaigns for many Fortune 500 corporations, delivering strategic business and marketing messages throughout the world.

Multi-disciplinary success led to network television writing and production contracts with CBS Television, Discovery Channels, and other international broadcast interests.

His interactions with presidents, prime ministers, and ministers of state has given him a perspective that serves him well as a fiction writer.

For more information, visit www.adamclaytonbooks. com

You can reach Adam at aclayton@adamclaytonbooks. com

Not Just Another Halloween
Denise DeVries

Every October, the Cat Lady ordered a bag of candy with her groceries. On the afternoon of the 31ˢᵗ, she poured the treats into a big bowl she kept near the front door. Then she sat in her rocking chair at the bay window and waited for the doorbell to ring. It never rang.

The deacon used the doorbell once a week when he brought Holy Communion. The Meals on Wheels people didn't even knock. They scuttled away without waiting to see if she retrieved the food. Church volunteers kept her walk clear but never approached her door. Even the mail carrier and delivery people dropped off packages without a sound. So, every Halloween, she checked the doorbell before she turned on the porch light. The Westminster Bells chimed clearly in her living room.

The visiting nurse rang the doorbell once a year and asked questions like, "What is your name?"

"Selma Wilkes," the Cat Lady answered. "It's right there on my bills and magazines."

"And your birth date?"

"I was born on October 31, 1939, in this very house. You know…"

The nurse interrupted before she could tell how her mama was all dressed for Mass when the labor pains came and was still wearing her hat when Selma was born.

"Any dizziness, lightheadedness, swollen ankles…?" It was the same every year.

After the nurse's visit, Selma would sit at her bay window as she did every afternoon, watching the seasons pass. Over the years, children grew and moved away, house paint faded, sidewalks were overtaken with weeds, and then the For Sale signs went up. Next came a procession of painters, renovators and lawn care companies, real estate agents in suits, and buyers of every type. New families moved in with young children, and Selma bought an extra bag of candy, just in case.

Every Halloween, the doorbell was silent. Selma's only companions were her cats. She lost count of all the kittens born under her porch and all the abandoned, sickly cats she had raised. Some repaid her by giving birth in unexpected places throughout the house.

As the leaves brightened on the gum tree and the days

became shorter, Selma began planning for Halloween. *This year*, she thought, *I'll carve a pumpkin and put it on the front porch…* As she wrote a list, a letter dropped from her mail slot into the basket underneath.

The return address was "Middle Peninsula Zoning Board." Selma looked at the page inside. "Official Citation for Animal Hoarding." Selma crumpled the paper into a ball and threw it to the cats.

That night, Selma dreamed of being dragged away in handcuffs as her cats were rounded up and exterminated. She awoke with her heart pounding, took out her rosary and prayed through a sleepless night. When dawn came, she got out of bed and searched her junk drawer for a marker. Then she made a big cardboard sign: "Free cats to a good home. Ring bell to enquire."

For the first time in months, or possibly years, Selma put on her outdoor shoes and hat, took her walker from the coat closet, and hobbled through the front yard. Cardinals swooped, gathered, and dispersed, their calls piercing the early morning silence. A few cats gathered around as she struggled to place the sign on her front gate. By the time she got back inside and took off her damp shoes, the neighborhood was beginning to stir. A yellow school bus stopped at the corner. A few cars drove past slowly as the drivers peered at her sign.

That day, the doorbell rang several times. Unfortunately, no one was there for a free cat. Selma's first visitor was a woman who had lived across the street for decades. "Shame on you," she said as Selma opened the door. "You can't give cats away for free. Don't you know people will take them away and eat them or worse?"

"What do you suggest I do?"

"Well, I don't know, but you can't give them away. People won't value something they get for free."

After the woman left, Selma went back out to her gate with a new sign: "Cats, $5 each. Ring to enquire."

She was just taking off her shoes when the doorbell rang again. Before she could open the door more than an inch, two angry voices overlapped.

"Selling cats!"

"Destroying the neighborhood…"

"…killing all the birds…"

Selma closed the door and turned the deadbolt. As she peeked out from behind her lace curtains, two red-faced women shouted through the closed door and the mail slot, punctuating their muffled words with an endless repetition of Big Ben's chimes. Selma turned her television on at full volume and retreated to the kitchen to make herself some tea. When her cup was empty, she went back to the front window and saw that the women had finally left. Only her torn and trampled sign lay where they had stood. She turned the TV down to what her mother would call "a dull roar" and picked up her shopping list. Her cats stared, disappointed, as she tore the paper into tiny pieces that fluttered into the trash container.

Selma started a new list. The afternoon sun fell onto her rocking chair, and she dozed until she heard the school bus braking at the corner. The group of parents who gathered at the bus stop seemed larger today. They stayed out talking even after the children went inside. Selma's oldest ginger cat, Big Mama, jumped onto the window seat for a better view. "Look, Big Mama. Some of those folks don't even have children at school. What are they doing?" One of the women pointed toward her house, and everyone turned to look. Selma moved back into the shadows.

When it was dark outside, Selma fed the outdoor cats, who had been waiting and pacing impatiently for more than an hour. "Sorry boys, we have to keep a low profile," she whispered. After supper, she stayed in the kitchen listening to the radio, then crept into her dark living room to watch the evening news. "Tomorrow is another day." She fell asleep after saying her prayers and didn't wake until the cats joined forces in the morning to coax her out of bed.

Just before lunch, the girl from the agency came through the kitchen door. Usually, when the weather was nice, Selma would sit out on the front porch while she cleaned. Today, she took a book to her room and tried to read. As soon as the book got interesting, the doorbell rang, startling the cat on her lap. "I am getting right tired of the sound of that bell," she muttered.

This time, her visitor was a man in a brown uniform. She stared through the screen, wondering if he was from UPS or the sheriff's office. He carried no packages or papers.

"Good morning, Ma'am, I'm with Middle Peninsula Animal Control." He waited, and when Selma didn't respond, he spoke louder. "Animal Control. We understand there's a situation here."

She crossed her arms and glared through the locked screen door. "My animals are fine and perfectly under control, thank you very much."

"Now, ma'am, I'm just here to help." He leaned down and lowered his voice. "There have been complaints."

Selma straightened to her full five feet in height and said, "I've a few complaints myself, young man. Rude and nosy neighbors for a start."

"Everything all right, Miz Wilkes?" The girl from the agency came in with her duster raised like a question mark.

"Certainly, dear, just a little kerfuffle over the kitties."

The young man at the door leaned in. "Is that you, Miz Jones?"

"Frank, what are you doing bothering Miz Wilkes?"

"I'm just trying to do my job. The neighbors are concerned about the number of cats here."

Selma turned to Mrs. Jones. "I'll handle this, dear. Don't forget to drop my list at the grocery store when you're finished." She unlocked the screen and opened it just enough to sidle through, closing the wooden door and then the screen behind her. "No need to broadcast my personal business, is there, uh, Frank?"

"No ma'am."

Selma took a hankie from her pocket and dusted off the two porch chairs. "Let's sit down and talk."

Frank remained standing, arms crossed. "I'm here to tell you your options. There's the trap and release program to prevent overpopulation, or I can give you the phone number of a pet rescue organization." He looked at the empty cat food dishes. "About how many cats are you feeding, ma'am?"

She flapped her hankie at him. "Goodness, I don't know. Those strays aren't my cats. I keep mine indoors. See, there's Big Mama in the window."

"And how many cats do you have inside?"

"How many am I allowed to have?"

He cleared his throat. "Do you have more than seven?"

"Inside? Certainly not. Why, they'd eat me out of house and home."

"I'll have to ask you to stop feeding the strays."

"But if I don't feed them, who will?"

Frank pulled a paper from his pocket. "Here's the number for the cat rescue organization. They'll help you."

Selma stood, took the paper, and looked up at the man in the brown uniform. "I assume our business is concluded. I'll just wait until you see yourself off my property."

"You will call them, won't you?"

"Goodbye. Make sure you close the front gate so it clicks." Selma watched until the man got in his brown truck and drove away. When she went inside, Mrs. Jones was washing the bay window with vinegar.

"I thought you girls didn't do windows."

"I was waiting for the dryer, so I decided to brighten your view for you."

"Please let yourself out when you finish. I have a headache and wish to rest in my room."

"Yes, ma'am."

Over the next few days, things seemed to be back to normal. The Meals on Wheels people left Selma's lunch and dinner on the porch. Only fliers and ads came through her mail slot until Thursday afternoon, when she received the Hull Crossing *Chronicle*. She took a brief glance at the front page, then put the paper on the end table to read later.

The next day, Father Winston came in person to deliver Communion. "How are you bearing up?" he asked when Selma opened the door. "I know this is a difficult time for you." He was holding a copy of the *Chronicle*. "I assume you read the letter to the editor."

"I haven't opened the paper yet. May I offer you some tea?"

"No thank you." He opened the newspaper. "I don't know what the editor was thinking, actually publishing your name and address along with all those accusations."

"Accusations?"

"I'm sorry to tell you, but one of your neighbors… Maybe you should read it for yourself." He held out the paper.

"My reading glasses are in the other room. Just go ahead and tell me."

He cleared his throat. "The headline is 'Cat Hoarding Horror.' This person claims that you're harboring dozens of feral cats, and they hint at everything from Satanic rituals to… How do I put this? Feline stew?"

Selma's laugh startled them both. Big Mama jumped onto the arm of her chair and peered into her face, which made her laugh even more. She took out her hankie and wiped her eyes. "Well, like my daddy always said, it's better to be talked about than ignored."

"I'm afraid there's more."

"More letters to the editor?"

"Actually, my secretary says you're on the internet." He pulled a phone from his pocket. "You've gone viral."

"But I'm as healthy as a horse."

"I mean, a photo of your house is circulating around the world and a lot of people are posting their opinions about keeping cats."

"Oh my! What can I do?"

Father Winston shook his head. "I really don't know. I suppose just stay inside until it all blows over."

"I always stay inside."

"Good. Be prepared to call the police if you feel threatened."

"I've got my daddy's old pistol."

The priest clutched his crucifix. "Why Selma! Surely you don't mean it."

"Just a little joke, Father."

"Oh, of course." He forced a chuckle. "Very humorous." Placing his hands on the arms of the chair, he half-stood. "I'd best be moving along."

"And my Communion?"

He sat back down. "Certainly, certainly. Now where did I put that kit?"

"Coffee table."

Father Winston calmed as he administered the Sacrament but left quickly after a brief prayer. As he let himself out, he said, "Lock that door behind me and call the police if anything happens. Anything at all."

"Yes, Father. I understand. Thank you." Selma turned the deadbolt, went to the bay window, and watched the priest go out the front gate. "Time to make another sign, I suppose." She repeated the process of the day before and posted the new sign on her picket fence. "No Trespassing!

BEWARE! Cat Lady is Armed!" She chuckled as she headed back inside. "Now they'll leave me alone."

This sign attracted even more attention. When the school bus arrived that afternoon, the high school students and even some parents stood on the sidewalk, holding up their phones to take photos. For the rest of the day, cars and curious pedestrians stopped in front of her house.

Selma followed her normal routine until bedtime. She took her father's pistol from the drawer in her bedside table and loaded it. "Just in case," she told her cats.

After a good night's sleep, Selma yawned, stretched, then looked at the calendar. "Tomorrow is my big day."

The next morning, Selma had her coffee and toast at the bay window. She and the cats watched the parade of photographers on the sidewalk. "It's better than TV."

The grocery boy was surrounded as he tried to open the gate. He waved off questions and rushed to the front door. He unfastened the screen and jumped when Selma opened the front door. Standing back in the shadows, she said, "Just set it down inside, dear."

It took Selma several trips to ferry everything to the kitchen. The cats turned the box into a playground as soon as she took out the first item. "No candy this year. I have something else in mind."

She took her stepladder from the front closet, set it up, got out a screwdriver, and tried to disconnect her doorbell. The box holding the mechanism had been painted over multiple times. Selma chipped away at the paint until her arms were tired but made little progress.

Selma spent the rest of the day watching the curious people gathered at the front gate. She followed her usual routine until bedtime, when she decided to skip the evening news and read her missal instead. Then she put the book back in the drawer with the loaded gun and turned off the light.

The next morning, despite her cats' insistence, she stayed in bed an extra half hour. "I won't be bossed on my special day." She didn't look out the front window until lunch. The street was empty. "I suppose my fame has run its course."

After lunch, Selma dusted off an old photo album and took it to her writing desk. She opened it at a ribbon marker close to the back, got out her magnifying glass, and read the caption. "My goodness! The last time I wore a costume was in 2019." She went backward through her memories of Halloween-themed birthdays, watching herself get younger. Finally, on the first page of the album, she found a studio photo of herself at age six. "No costume and no mask, just me." She looked at it for a long time. "I always wanted a pretty pink cake with roses and a dress to match. Instead, it was black cats, spiders, goblins and ghouls."

That evening, for the first Halloween she could

remember, Selma kept the porch light off and didn't check the bell. After supper, she put on her best church dress and hat. She took the pistol and set it on the table by the locked door. When the chimes sounded, she was in the kitchen. She crossed the dark living room, surrounded by glowing eyes, and looked outside.

Trick-or-treaters were standing at the door and lined up past the gate. "Too late now," she muttered. "There's no candy this year." As she turned to head back to the kitchen, the bell rang again. And again.

"That's quite enough!" She couldn't hear herself over the chimes. She switched on the entry hall light and picked up the pistol. Someone pushed the doorbell again. Slowly, as if she were in a dream, Selma aimed.

"BLAM!"

After the echoes died away, there was a moment of silence. Inside, the cats blinked in their hiding places. Outside, as if the world had been holding its breath, screams, shouts and the thunder of running feet all burst forth at once. Then silence fell again.

Two police officers found Selma at the kitchen table. Several cats slunk into dark corners, licking their whiskers. A spent candle still smoked in the remains of a pink, rose-covered birthday cake.

Selma blinked at the officers in their protective gear. "If I'd known you were coming I'd've got a bigger cake."

"Are you all right, ma'am?"

She wiped her lips with an embroidered napkin. "Just a little trouble with the doorbell. Daddy's old pistol took care of that."

One officer lifted her helmet visor. "We'll need to file a report, ma'am. Can you tell us exactly what happened?"

"Certainly. You see, I just realized it after all these years." She looked up at the officers.

"Yes ma'am, you realized…"

"I've been celebrating the wrong thing."

About the Author

Translator and poet Denise DeVries returned to fiction writing after joining the Tempe Public Library writing workshops in 2017. In 2019, Denise moved back to the rural Virginia town that inspired *Hull Crossing Chronicles*, her historical fiction series, and *Key to History*, her middle grade time travel books. She wrote the one-act plays *A Two-Faced Spinster* and *Barbershop Gossip* in honor of Tempe Library Readers Theater, of which she was a member for one season. The characters and situations in the plays are inspired by her fiction.

You can find out more at www.denisedevriesauthor. wordpress.com.

The Graveyard

Sandy Hicks

Deep in the forest, beyond the farmhouse and long since forgotten, sat a graveyard, overgrown with grasses and creepers from years of neglect. In the summer the natural world buzzed around the crumbling stone markers as hummingbirds and bees sipped nectar from the flaxen honeysuckle flowers, whose vines grew rampant in the warming sun. Grasshoppers thrived, springing about at times and mumbling in loud, low buzzing vibrations at others. As the sun slid across the sky, the rabbits hid in cool burrows nestled against the gravestones. During the summer days the dead rested, entertained by the goings on above their decayed bodies. As fall approached, though, their spirits became restless. In the cooling nights they sought warmth that could never be felt again or the company of the living that could not be had.

The dead in this graveyard were not haunters or ghosts seeking revenge for some egregious acts of violence committed against them. Most in life were wheat farmers, some had had small holdings in the planting and export of tobacco, and a few were craftsmen of the barrels that shipped out of Yorktown, Virginia, full of the labors of the farmers. The land they now rested in was inherited from their ancestors, who crossed the ocean in perilous wooden boats and whom they eventually joined in this iron-fence bound plot. Many years had gone by since the last of this community had been laid to rest. The decomposers of the soil had completed their mission of breaking down the wooden caskets, and the roots of the oaks had long since used the nourishment within to grow to towering heights with massive branches that just barely touched each other as the wind whistled by.

They were all content in the world they occupied. But, when the full moon rose to illuminate the forest and the bright stars shone through the nearly bare branches of the trees in fall, the souls of the dead left their resting bodies and came to the surface to the world of the living. Without bones or body mass, everyone had the ability to move as they pleased. On this night, they were celebrating the harvest moon. A hoedown dance began with the bellowing of the bullfrogs blended with the whippoorwill's snappy song and the owl's occasional forlorn hooting. Even the trees got involved as the soft wind blew and clapped their branches like hands with unpleasantly long fingers, adding to the sense of weird deadness with life that permeated the forest whenever the nonliving emerged.

Forming a circle, the spirits began. Swooshing this way for a turn and then that way, they stamped the earth in unseen buckle-strap shoes and swirled in swishy skirts. With a do-si-do and a promenade, the men donned perceived hats while the ladies laughed with joy, and the children, who had passed from horrific diseases, ran amongst them. All had such a fabulous time, many forgot their untimely demise or were thankful for it after having walked the earth for nearly a century. As twilight approached, one by one they sank back to their earthly habitats and slept again.

All except one.

She had been young without a bright future when her tragic life ended. Covered in the pox, she suffered long and painfully. Her bones, left in the graveyard, were deformed such that she barely walked when living, so eaten away with lesions caused by the virus. For weeks she had cried until the angel of death finally heard her shallow voice and rode up in a polished black carriage, pulled by massive obsidian horses. She was happy to leave her earthly body but watched with sadness as her mother screamed and wept, damning whoever brought this terrible disease to their small village of Yorktown.

On this bright morning, the young girl was attracted to booming sounds coming from the river that had started in the darkness of the night. Their vibrations reverberated through the forest, causing the trees to shudder. A slight breeze rustled the colorful leaves as she left the forest and drifted across an expansive field dug with redoubts. The siege had raged for weeks, but she had only been slightly aware of it and its sounds, being six feet under. On the surface, the earsplitting booms of cannons along with the vociferous cries of soldiers, both living and dying, were deafening. She stopped and stared.

She moved quickly through the field, her interest drawn to the river and the battle on its cliffs and on the large wooden ships bobbing on the water. One group was being cornered into an area near the village and on the banks of the York River. The soldiers were preparing an escape across to the land on the other side. Men in red wool coats erratically ran past the cooper's shop, through the trees and down the alley known by the locals as Tobacco Road. In her lifetime, huge barrels of exports rolled down this path to waiting ships below. On this day, musket balls flew by and cannons screamed, ejecting massive cast iron balls. The scene was one of agony. As she watched, the startled souls of the dead peeled from their earthly bodies in confusion. In the river, ships groaned as their wood was blasted into splinters from mortar fire and sank. Men amassed from them like angry ants, mostly to drown, their souls emerging as a dense fog. Some of the ships were destroyed and sunk on purpose to keep the Americans from commandeering them. The scene was hell.

The battle raged as she stood among the men, not to be perceived by the frantic living and suddenly to be seen by the recent dead. Future American and French commanders yelled orders that were quickly translated to a melody by the young fifer and drummer as the forces moved against each other; clashing, ripping, gnawing at life. Bayonets gutted the living as hand-to-hand combat ensued. This battle seemed lost for the future Americans as the British ran to boats waiting on the shore, their only escape. In the chaos, few were aware of the storm that brewed offshore.

The spirits of the soldiers watched the battle of Yorktown from newfound perspectives and became aware of the strategy of the enemy. Massive clouds began to climb into the sky, full of moisture and wicked winds aided by unseen forces. Soldiers in both life and death, they gathered their strength to build the fierce storm, throwing lightning and producing capsizing winds on the York. The British could not escape to Gloucester for fear of sinking. Their strategy foiled, they were forced to surrender, losing the final battle of the Revolutionary War.

In the aftermath of the devastation, as the British Empire stood humiliated and defeated by a determined and driven group of newfound Americans in search of freedom, the exhausted young girl made her way back to her family in a graveyard long since forgotten by the living. The new spirits of the dead soldiers watched her leave, standing proudly behind Washington as he acknowledged the surrender of the British and celebrated the end to the terrible war. They wept dry tears while the fifer's melody meandered across the battlefields and stepped gently over their decomposing bodies.

About the Author

A native Virginian, Sandy received her degree in education and taught children most of her career. During this time, she composed poems and short stories that explored the natural world in an effort to show the next generation the value of such things. She is currently working on a collection of poems about the seaside and an anthology of short stories that take place in the forests of the Chesapeake Bay watershed. In addition to writing, she paints in watercolors and acrylics and has works in several local galleries.

All Hallows' Eve At Rosewell

Patti Gaustad Procopi

"**H**urry up. We need to get the cars emptied and the tents set up before dark," the camp counselor Jenny called out.

Beth grabbed a box and headed toward the campsite. This is going to be so cool, she told herself. Spending Halloween camping at the ruins of Rosewell Plantation. There weren't that many cool things in Gloucester. It was actually a pretty boring place to grow up. They'd shut down the skating rink and the bowling alley, so if you didn't play sports, you had nothing to do.

Setting the box down, Beth headed back to the parking lot to grab more supplies. But the sight of the once magnificent building caught her eye, and she stopped and stared. The walls rose three stories up to the sky, and at each corner over the remains were massive chimneys. Beth wished she could climb to the third floor and look out the window across to the river. But there were no floors left. Just walls.

She would have liked to have seen it in its heyday, imagining the glittering rooms and beautiful people sweeping in and out with servants carrying drinks and food for all the guests. Unfortunately, Rosewell had burned down in 1916. Reports at the time said the flames and smoke could be seen as far away as Williamsburg, across the York River.

Re-focusing on the task at hand, Beth ran to the van and grabbed a tent. She tried to carry two but they were too heavy, so she settled on taking one. Little by little the vans emptied out and the campsite filled up. The counselors divided the kids into smaller groups, each responsible for setting up a tent. The tents were set up in a circle. There were four tents and each slept five—four kids and one camp counselor per tent. The kids rolled out their sleeping bags inside their tent and put their personal items on top of their bags. Then the campers and counselors gathered around the fire pit in the middle.

"First thing we should do is decide what we want for dinner," Frank, the head counselor, said.

This announcement was greeted by a chorus of voices shouting, "Hotdogs, beans, s'mores," and other more impractical suggestions such as tacos and ice cream.

Frank laughed. "Yes to all of that. We can cook hotdogs on sticks over the fire and heat up beans. And for dessert…" He paused dramatically until they all shouted, "S'mores!"

"Yes to that as well," he said.

Each tent was given a task: gather firewood, find hot dog sticks, arrange s'more ingredients, and set up drinks. Soon there was a roaring fire, and each camper had a hot dog roasting on a stick.

Beth was enjoying herself, but she was also feeling a little down because her best friend since kindergarten had recently moved away. She and Lindy had met on their first day of kindergarten and became instant BFFs. Since that day, they spent almost every waking moment together. Their mothers even joked that they must have been twins, mysteriously separated at birth. This of course was absurd because they looked nothing alike. Beth was blonde and blue-eyed, with skin so pale it burned at the mention of the word sun, while Lindy had curly brown hair, brown eyes, and soft mocha-brown skin. Beth always envied Lindy's skin. How nice it must be to have a permanent tan.

Lindy's family had moved to Williamsburg because her father thought the schools were better over there. And even though it was just across the river, it might as well have been a million miles away. The river was wide, and Beth had neither a car nor a boat to go visit. Their mothers still made sure they got together occasionally but it wasn't the same. The occasions now seemed to be less and less frequent as Lindy made new friends at her new school.

Beth's mother had signed her up for weekend camp, hoping the variety of activities would engage Beth and help her find a new best friend. She liked being busy and learning new things. She particularly liked history and hoped to be a history teacher one day. Fortunately, there was a lot of history in Gloucester, even if there was a severe lack of entertainment of more modern kinds.

The sun set while dinner was being cooked. All the kids went to their tents to get hoodies to keep warm against the cooling air. Virginia in the fall could be quite cold. As they snuggled closer to the fire, now came Beth's favorite part of camping: ghost stories. Both Jenny and Frank were great story tellers and Beth could listen to them forever.

First they gave the kids a brief history of Rosewell Plantation. Beth learned that Rosewell was built by the Pages, one of the most powerful and wealthy families in Virginia in the early colonial days. The house was built to rival the Governor's Palace in Williamsburg. Beth remembered visiting that with Lindy on one of their get-togethers. Rosewell was larger than any other home in Virginia at the time. While the family lived there for almost a hundred years, they eventually became strapped for cash and had to sell the house.

"In addition to the family, the estate had many enslaved people who worked as field hands, house servants, maids, and cooks," Frank said. "Plantations in those days had to be self-sufficient." He paused. "Does anyone know what that means?"

Hands shot up, including Beth's. She wasn't one hundred percent sure of the answer but she was sure she knew more than the other kids. Frank called on Sam, who suddenly mumbled and stumbled and couldn't answer the question. After selecting another kid who also had no idea, Frank answered the question himself.

"In those days, houses were very far apart. There were no stores that people could run out to or restaurants if they didn't feel like cooking, or even any DoorDash." That brought a laugh from all the kids. "They had to grow all their own food and then trade for things they couldn't grow, like tea. Many of the slaves performed skilled trades like blacksmithing, woodworking, butchering. They raised all the vegetables and produce for the farm."

Frank looked around. "Even though Rosewell burned down almost fifty years after the Civil War, the descendants of those enslaved people cheered when they heard the house was burning."

Beth grimaced. It bothered her that anyone would cheer for the destruction of such a beautiful place. Slavery was awful but it was over by the time Rosewell burned.

Slumping a little lower, Beth remembered arguments she and Lindy had about those kinds of things. Lindy always ended them by saying, "You don't understand. Your ancestors weren't enslaved." And what could Beth say to that? Nothing. Once she complained to her mother about Lindy's attitude.

"It's like I can't win but seriously, the war ended like over a hundred and fifty years ago. And it's not like Lindy was a slave or her parents or even her grandparents. Things are great now. We all live together and nobody cares about who your ancestors were or what they did."

"It's more complicated than that," her mom said. "Even after slavery ended, Black people still suffered. I suggest you two talk about something else."

Frank was pointing out where they thought the outbuildings and homes of the enslaved people stood. "There were even two separate graveyards. One for the family in the main house and one for the servants and slaves. The family cemetery had elaborate marble tombstones. There were hardly any headstones in the other graveyard. Often enslaved people had no names other than their first and their master's last name as theirs."

Jenny interrupted. "But enough history." All the kids cheered. "Let's make some s'mores and then settle down for the good, scary stories. It's Halloween night, after all!"

After the s'mores were eaten and the trash and debris

collected and put in trash bags, the kids once again settled around the fire.

"Does anyone know what tonight is?" Jenny asked.

Ben said, "That's easy. It's Halloween and we're not getting any candy!"

Everyone laughed at that.

"But where does the word 'Halloween' come from?" Jenny asked the circle.

They all shrugged and looked at each other.

"Hundreds of years ago this night was called All Hallows' Eve, not Halloween," Jenny said. "It was a night for remembering the dead not for collecting candy. Tomorrow is All Saints' Day, which was a feast to remember saints and Christian martyrs."

Frank took up the story. "Over time, All Hallows' Eve morphed into Halloween." He stretched out the words. "Hallows… eve into Hallow… een."

"I get it," someone said.

"But before the Christians, there were other people in the world who often celebrated the seasons. The Celts in particular celebrated a harvest festival called Samhain, which had pagan roots. And some people even believe that Christians superimposed their feast day of All Hallows' Eve on top of Samhain to Christianize the day and the people," Jenny explained.

"What is the connection?" Frank paused, looking around the circle. "Dead people!" he said in a deep, scary voice. "All Hallows' Eve was dedicated to remembering the dead. But Halloween became a celebration of horror and the supernatural. It was believed in the early church that souls of the departed wandered the earth until All Saints' Day and the evening before, All Hallows' Eve, provided the dead with one last chance to gain vengeance before they moved on to the next life. This developed into people wearing masks or costumes to disguise themselves from the dead. Many Christians believed that once a year, on Hallowe'en, the dead within the churchyards rose up and danced in one last wild and hideous carnival. This was to remind people not to forget the end of all things earthly."

Jenny took up the story. "Today's Halloween customs are thought to have been influenced by the Celts through the celebration of Samhain, which marked the end of harvest and the beginning of the dark days of winter. The boundary between worlds thinned, and spirits could more easily come into this world. Some of these celebrations included people going house to house in costume, reciting verses in exchange for food. Some of them blackened their faces with ashes from bonfires and threatened mischief if they were not given food or a treat."

"In those days, Jack-o'-lanterns were made from turnips, not pumpkins, which were not known at the time. The carved lanterns with grotesque faces were said to be used to ward off evil spirits. The Scots and the Irish had traditions which most closely resemble modern Halloween. They brought those customs with them when they emigrated to this country and eventually Halloween as we know it evolved. It's interesting to know where these kinds of things come from," Frank concluded.

"And now for a scary story, because what's Halloween without a scare," Jenny said.

She began a story about a boy who dressed up on Halloween not to trick-or-treat or get candy but to terrorize the neighborhood. Beth leaned her head on her knees as she listened and soon Jenny's voice sounded far away. Beth felt like she was sleeping but at the same time she thought she was wide awake. She tried to open her eyes to make sure she was still at the fire with the other campers, but she could not force them open. Jenny's voice faded and Beth began to hear music. Kind of like the music at church with old-fashioned instruments. After a few minutes, she finally opened her eyes. She was standing outside a window at Rosewell. The plantation was no longer a ruin but a beautiful building.

Glancing in the window, she realized she was looking into the ballroom. She remembered Frank telling them Rosewell had often been the scene of fabulous balls and parties in the past. And she was seeing it. How could she be seeing it? The music floated through the air and gorgeous gowns twirled and danced in front of her. The women were all beautiful, the men handsome, the candles burned bright, and the walls glittered like diamonds. Suddenly the music began to slow, as if on the wrong speed. The dancing couples turned more slowly and the faces that passed by were skeletons. Dancing skeletons. She covered her mouth to stop from screaming and turned away.

Stumbling from the horrible scene, Beth tried to calm her breathing. She needed to find the campsite and the others. They wouldn't believe what she had seen, and she'd have to drag them back to the house. Tearing through the trees, she soon became completely disoriented. She had no idea where the campsite was. She turned back to the house but in the moonlight, it had faded into a ruin again. Was she dreaming? No, she was completely wide awake. This was not a dream.

Music began to play in front of her. It was not the same music that had come from the house. This was simple. A banjo, possibly, and drums? Walking slowly forward, Beth entered a clearing. She realized she must be in the slave quarters. The houses were tiny. The people dressed in simple patched clothing. Food was cooking over a fire but there was no abundance like up at the main house. A woman, crying, held a tiny bundle in her arms.

"You have to let her go now Selma," a voice said. A man put his arm around the woman and the people started walking through the woods. They came to another clearing where there was a small hole dug in the ground.

"Anybody going to give my baby a headstone? With her name? She deserves that much," the woman cried.

"Yes. It's there already."

Beth saw a flat piece of wood with a name written in charcoal. She knew it would not last through a season of rain.

The woman knelt and laid the bundle in the grave and gently covered it with her hands. "All our people going back to the first one are here and no one even knows. Their names erased. Their stories erased. We just going to be erased too. While the folks in the big house get their marble headstones and will live forever."

"No, Selma. We might not have marble headstones but we will live forever because our children's children's children will know what happened here. They won't forget," an ancient man said to the woman.

As the people stood to walk back to their homes, their faces disappeared and skeletons walked past Beth, so close she could have touched them.

She thought about Lindy and her anger over the house and what had happened and how her ancestors were treated and Beth felt sick. She had not understood.

Beth woke to Jenny rubbing her back and asking if she was okay.

Sitting up, Beth saw she was outside the tent, lying on the ground. She shook her head. "I'm fine…" she muttered, though she wasn't sure if she was.

"Why were you sleeping out here? I thought I made sure everyone was tucked up in the tents."

"I think I had to go to the bathroom…" Beth mumbled. "I guess I was tired and just…" Beth struggled to come up with a rational reason.

"Come on silly, we're going to take a nature walk along the river," Jenny said.

Everyone started exiting the tents to cook breakfast. The dreams from last night came rushing back. But she knew they weren't dreams. She had seen the souls of the dead on All Hallows' Eve.

About the Author

Patti Gaustad Procopi is a former army brat who lived all over the world before settling in Gloucester, Virginia, with her husband Greg. They raised three daughters and numerous cats and dogs.

Patti worked at two area history museums for thirty-two years. After retiring, she finally had the time to do the thing she always wanted to do: write!

Patti's writing is about emotional connections, friendship and family. Her first novel, *Please...Tell Me More*, was published in 2020 by Blue Fortune Enterprises, LLC, followed by *I'll Get By, Stop Talking*, and *The Murderer You Know*, a podcast mystery.

Patti has had stories printed in literary journals and anthologies and read on a podcast. She's given talks at area libraries and writing symposiums about how to tell your story.

When not writing, Patti enjoys photographing birds on her creek. She also enjoys gardening, yoga, and researching her family genealogy.

You can find Patti's books on Barnes & Noble, Amazon, or wherever books are sold, and you can contact her on her website, pattiproauthor.com, or email patti.pro@cox.net or on Facebook.

In Death, We Don't Part

allison keli

Our *First Anniversary*

On that crisp Halloween night, Meri stood by the sea. As her hair danced in the chilly breeze, the light from the gibbous moon cast its glow about her shoulders. The ocean waves continued to crash, breaking at her feet. Meri's nose twitched at the whiff on the wind. The scent was seagrass mixed with the musk of a cologne she knew so well. She half-turned to greet her husband as he gently padded on the sand towards her, his arms and hands outstretched, his mouth upturned in a smile.

This was the one year anniversary of their wedding.

The First Time We Met

One early evening at the start of an August, Meri

and her friend, Ruthie, were jogging down the Virginia Beach boardwalk. From start to finish, the boardwalk was a staggering three miles long and bespeckled with the glistening sand that lay just below its concrete. A small median divided the paths for bicycles and leg-powered buggies from the walkers and runners on the boardwalk.

As they ran, the shining sun on the left had started to dip behind the tall edifices, the hotels and motels and eateries. The sun's shadow created a slight summer chill. After the girls passed the looming King Neptune cast-bronze statue on their right, they continued until they reached the boardwalk's end.

Their plan was to turn around and head back toward the thirty-four-foot Neptune after a brief walking break. Families were still heavily vacationing this time of year, but locals were milling around as well. Public benches were often claimed by the unhoused, who slept there during the summer. This time of day, and the time of year, the boardwalk was fully involved with the bustle of human activity.

After they turned back toward Neptune, the hotels and smaller offbeat ice cream shops hidden in the shadows were now on their right. Carts selling shaved ice or frozen coffee drinks begged tourists for a sale. Despite the separate path for faster-moving patrons, skateboards and bicycles passed them.

A final glance to the left side of the boardwalk revealed

one of many cascading staircases that led to the large beach. Each block had its own entrance to the sea. The ocean beckoned late-day surfers, post-dinner swimmers, and sandcastle builders. Umbrellas dotted the landscape.

As they reached Neptune's trident, their leg muscles began to twitch. They did not plan to stop again until they reached the 8th street exit to their reward—the famous *Orange Slush* drink delivered by a bartender at their favorite hot spot, *The Hut*. Games, drinks, snacks and more, this outdoor pub was a beloved locale to unwind.

They started their final sprint by dodging between families taking selfies with the stoic Neptune. *This really is too busy of a spot to jog*, Meri thought. No sooner had the thought exited her mind did she, quite suddenly and *very* forcefully, get pushed. Someone shouted, and as she stumbled to safety from a child on his rogue bicycle, her friend's concerned face only half-registered. Looking up, her rescuer stood over her, with a slight remaining halo of sun around his head. He appeared unreal, as an angel might.

Ruthie ran up behind her and grabbed her by the shoulders, shaking. "Oh my God, if that kid had run into you, you would have been a mangled mess on the ground!"

The rescuer's face broke into a casual smile, brushing off his noted incredulous save by the friend. Meanwhile,

Meri was *violently* enchanted by him. As her breath slowed, her astonishment turned to unease as something was *so* familiar about him, something so comforting… Was that it? Not exactly safe, but… *right*.

Yet, she was positive she had never met this man before in her life.

He extended his hand, green eyes now dimming to hazel as the sun made its last plunge behind the buildings. "My name is Brendan."

Ruthie extended her own hand, warmly laughing. "Hi, I'm Ruthie, and the speechless one you saved is Meri, of the Sea, if you will."

Meri, finally, hesitatingly so, painted a smile onto her face. She gripped his hand, feeling a steady touch underneath her sweaty palm. "My name means *sea*." She paused for a second. "Oh, I'm so sorry," she quickly added, wiping her palms on her shorts, recoiling in slight horror about the wetness.

"No worries," he replied, looking into her eyes. "Have we met before?"

She paused, knowing the answer, and feeling ill at ease that he asked. "I don't think so. Are you from around here?"

"No." He gestured toward the ocean. "I'm from here, I'm from there."

"Navy?" asked Ruthie.

He smiled, confirming her assessment. As they fell in

step with one another, Meri recognized that he had never really answered her question. With no distinguishable accent she could ascertain, he may have been from nowhere at all.

"Well, thanks again for saving my friend," said Ruthie, wrapping her arm around Meri. "But hey, we could also get your number and buy you a drink! As a thank you?"

"Or leave it to chance to meet again," murmured Meri, feeling uneven.

"Really, no need. I just saw that kid making a beeline for you, so I intervened. I promise, all is well. You two have a good jog! Maybe I'll run into you again, right? Leave it to fate."

Ruthie giggled and pinched Meri's arm. There was no way Brendan had heard Meri, yet he was echoing what she had said. With final smiles, the two ran off, leaving him in the motel's shadow.

The Next Time We Met

Several weeks later, the scent of autumn was encroaching. Tourism was still booming, but something in the atmosphere had shifted. Labor Day, one of the busiest holidays for Virginia Beach, was behind them, and local children had returned to school and were missing from the mayhem.

Meri grabbed her *Blue Merlin* smoothie bowl from the counter of *The Green Kitty*, a local café. She walked outside to the covered picnic tables. Consisting of a medley of banana, vanilla, blueberry and granola, the bowl's contents were some of Meri's favorite flavors. She stretched out her long, lean legs underneath one of the tables, pulled a book out of her bag, and slid her sunglasses further back on top of her head.

While the evening was young, she hadn't felt like going for her traditional post-work jog on the boardwalk. She was going to relax with her book and smoothie, then slip into her car and drive home. She lived close to the oceanfront, a short distance up Shore Drive.

She tried balancing her spoon with one hand while reading with the other. She was alone; all the other people were inside the café. She was so entranced by her story that the people coming and going did not bother her. She snorted with a character in her book and instantly lifted her head in surprise. Some of the granola had been sucked down the wrong tube, and she vigorously started coughing, trying to force it out. A nearby man was afraid she was choking, so he came up behind her to do an abdominal thrust.

At the last moment, she managed to catch her breath, embarrassed the man had rushed over to her. "I'm fine, thank you," she said, looking up at him. Her eyes dropped to the ground in disbelief before traveling upwards again to his twinkling eyes. "I know for *sure* we have met before," he said with a smile.

She couldn't help but laugh, a feeling of warmth spreading across her abdomen as she realized who her would-be savior was.

"Do you go around saving others from harm, or is it just me?"

He slid into the chair next to her. "It's just you. For some reason, it's just you."

'Til Death Do Us Part

The whirlwind romance astonished all of Meri's friends. She had never dated much, usually choosing to hang out with her friends as the third wheel. She'd never had any inclination to get married or have a family. Her focus had been either on her work at a nonprofit or on having fun. But suddenly having this partner-in-crime, this person who was *always* with her, her friends were noticeably alarmed.

Even so, nobody felt *too* distressed. Brendan was a really nice man, after all, and easy on the eyes, too. Mostly, though, there was nothing tangible to put their fingers on. He wasn't rude. He didn't argue. He wasn't controlling or forceful.

Although Meri was initially unsettled, these feelings drifted away as their love affair continued. In fact, she loved him more than she had ever loved anyone.

They were in sync and rotated around one another as if in a gravitational pull or a magnetic field. Meri eventually learned that Brendan was from a small family farm somewhere in the Northeast. He was an only child, and his mother had died when he was young. His father, and mostly his grandparents, had been the ones to raise him. He had been brought to the area by the Navy but was no longer employed by them. Meri never pushed the issue. He was now working as a welder.

Much to the chagrin of Meri's family and friends, when he asked her to marry him, there was no stopping the tornado. They were inseparable, seemingly unable to survive without the other. They were so intertwined nobody expected them to attend any events without the other. Meri's friends would not even ask her to jog without Brendan.

It was assumed they were together. Always.

About three months past the year mark of their first meeting, they married on the beach just behind Neptune. It was a perfect autumn evening at the beach. Warm enough to be barefoot, yet chilly enough to wear a light jacket.

As it was Halloween, Meri's friends had crafted a small walkway of smiling jack-o'-lanterns and other squashes leading to an archway. The bride and groom stood where the wet sand met up with the dry sand as they exchanged their vows. While most of the attendees were friends or family of Meri's, Brendan was able to conjure some friends for the event.

In Death

Through the winter and spring of the following year, the two remained inseparable. When one was off and the other had to go to work, the worker would have a ride. When both worked, they tried to carpool. They never wanted to be away from each other too long. They hadn't had time to honeymoon, so they considered every day a part of their honeymoon. They had plenty of local areas to explore as newlyweds—First Landing State Park on bicycles, hitching a boat to the Middle Ground Lighthouse in the James River, or any historical place on the peninsula.

Almost a year upon having first met, they were paddling near a rocky point jutting out into the sea. While Brendan surfed, Meri would often paddleboard with the dolphins and other sea life. A mid-season hurricane was ravaging the seas by Bermuda, and due to its proximity, some of the swells had started to trickle inward from the horizon toward the coast.

Red flags were hung along the walkways leading to the beach, a clear warning sign of danger ahead, but Brendan wasn't worried. Meri, however, began having a hard time staying away from the craggy rocks. With Brendan merely fifty feet from her, riding one of the larger waves of the morning, the first taste of fear overwhelmed Meri.

Her arm slammed into a rock, and blood began to ooze from a deep scrape. Meri muttered to herself, knowing she needed to pull up onto the rocks to stay safe. It was her only option. She glanced at the rocks and saw the sea spray creating a slippery shelf. It wasn't the safest thing to do, but she figured it was her best option as she could not manage the ocean any longer.

She shouted to Brendan, spitting out seawater, trying to get across to him what her plans were. He yelled back, now less than twenty-five feet away. He was close enough that Meri could sense his rising alarm. Their situation was growing more precarious by the moment.

"Meri!" he yelled, his voice carrying on the wind. "Not safe!"

Even so, she pulled herself up onto the rock, the strong, unrelenting wind blowing her wet hair off of her shoulders. The ocean leapt up, grabbed her paddleboard, and ripped it out of her hands. Her choice was to let the board go or get tossed into the rocks like a rag doll.

At the last moment, she let go of the board, throwing her hands up into the air to fully release it. She looked over at Brendan, now only fifteen feet away, furiously trying to paddle to rescue her, yet again.

The look of surprise on his face after a quick glance to his left toward the monster wave set to swallow him was like no other. In matched terror, Meri met his eyes one last time. The howl of the sea and scream of the wind melded into a roar and then, sand and ocean blinding her in a rage, Brendan disappeared into the blue of the sea.

In slow motion, his board flew upwards before smashing down onto him.

Meri screamed, screamed with the wind as Brendan's lifeless form repeatedly smashed against the rocks she was now stranded on. She reached down to pull his body up, his neck at an angle that no living being could have. His eyes were blankly open, his mouth slightly parted.

By then, the other surfers who had been nearby, well aware of the rapidly deteriorating situation, had rushed to their aid. Unfortunately for Brendan, he no longer needed any assistance.

While his body was limp on the rocks, Brendan's spirit floated next to Meri. The draw behind him was a warm, pulsating glow. However, it gripped slightly less than the pull from the agony of watching his loved one suffer.

He could not leave her.

He would not leave her.

We Don't Part

When Meri and Brendan first met, they felt like they knew one another. He saved her multiple times, but she was not able to save him. Although she felt his presence, she became depressed and stopped doing all the things she loved. Eventually, though, as she knew he was there with her, she started to speak with him. She started to resume doing all the things they had done together.

And so, they roamed the earth, one without form,

and one *with* form. Her friends thought she had lost her mind, still referring to her husband in the present. While they pointed out how unhealthy it was, pushing therapy, pushing meds, pushing *anything* to help, she finally clammed up and refused to talk about it anymore.

Halloween night had returned, their one year wedding anniversary. Her friends tried to occupy her with a dinner, but she told them she was fine, that she wanted a quiet night by herself.

Only she wasn't alone.

When she placed her hand in Brendan's, by the sea, of the sea, her body fell flaccid behind her. To those who witnessed the odd occurrence, Meri had walked up to the crashing waves, stretched out her hand, smiled eerily in the moonlight, then simply collapsed to the earth.

allison keli loves Halloween so much, she actually got married on October 31st... in Salem, Massachusetts... during a blue moon... by a green witch... at Ropes Mansion, aka Allison's house from *Hocus Pocus*!

allison is a STEM educator, bodyworker and workshopper. Her varied interests have led her to write on numerous topics. As a massage therapist, she writes about holistic health and spiritual themes at www.SwellnessVibes.com. As a mom, she writes about parenting at www.FlightoftheSeedling.Wordpress.com.

Her books include a children's fantasy/science mash-up about the Perseid Meteor Shower. In *Phenix & Fox: Shooting Stars*, her young son helped create some of the illustrations. Her adult magical realism series, *The Light Thrower*, currently contains two full-length novels: *When Violet Got Bored* and *When Violet Took Flight*. Full of humor and kitschy pop culture references, the novels tackle hard questions about destiny and free will.

allison's semi-historical spookfests, *The Hauntings of DoG Street*, started as a series on the now defunct Kindle Vella. The third novella in the series, *The Wren Building*, will be published in the fall of 2025. The first two novellas, *Chowning's Tavern* and *Bruton Parish Church*, introduce us to a college student who discovers she has a knack for speaking with 18th century ghosts who still have stories to tell.

allison lives in SE Virginia with her two kitties, rising middle schooler son, and firefighting husband. Visit her at www.allisonkeli.com for more fun and mayhem!

The Enchantment
Ginger Adelstone

Samantha sat at her desk in the upstairs nook she had created as a private space to grade her students' papers. She and her husband Darryl and daughter Lizzie lived in a small, Cape Cod-style cottage on the James River. The view was spectacular, and she often imagined what it must have been like a few hundred years ago, when goods were shipped via the river.

She finished grading her eighth-grade English class tests and was trying to devise a project that would create a friendly class competition. School was only in its second week, and she was hoping to deviate from the prescribed work to better engage the students.

The end of the day, for her, was about family. Her husband Darryl had made dinner, and Hugo, their terrifying Dachshund, dashed toward her. Lizzie, probably following the scent of the food, came around the corner from her room. She was now fifteen, almost ready to start driving. Sam walked into the kitchen and gave a happy sigh. "What's for dinner? It smells great." Darryl beamed. "Fried catfish, pepper cheese biscuits, and coleslaw," he said.

"Easy and always a hit," Sam said.

They settled in for dinner, and Darryl asked Sam about her students. "I like the class this year," she said. "A few of them are very smart, and I don't want them to lose interest. I'm thinking about giving an extra credit assignment to stretch their thinking skills."

Darryl and Sam discussed what type of project she could present, and Lizzie piped up. "What about a short history of their family tree and how they ended up in Virginia?"

Sam beamed at her daughter. "What a terrific idea! Of course it will be optional, because not everyone wants to know about their family." That night, she put together an outline of what the project would entail and printed it out.

The next morning, when Sam entered her classroom, the students were seated and somewhat quiet. Before she began talking about dangling participles, the lesson for the day, Sam announced the extra-credit project.

Several of the girls were very excited to start

questioning their parents about their family history and see what information they could uncover.

Cynthia was from a wealthy family; her father, a local attorney, now worked for the District Attorney's office. There were rumors that her dad was being considered to run for an upcoming Senate seat. Before dinner, her dad, Steven, grilled on the patio and lit the fire pit. Cynthia loved whenever her father did this. She and her parents would sit by the glow of the flames, chatting for hours.

As Cynthia and her mom sat talking, her dad grilled the steaks. Cynthia brought up the extra-credit project. "This will be fun," she said to her mom. "I think Mrs. Wilson came up with a great idea. Do you have any information about our family, like the year they arrived in America or their exact arrival date? Or how they got here?"

Her mother, Gayle, froze. "I'll see what I can find," she said. Truthfully, she had quite a bit of history on both families and how they arrived in this country, their struggles and challenges of being different. How much should she share with her daughter? She hoped her daughter would be too excited to notice her fearful reaction. She quickly changed the subject, and they chatted about Cynthia's upcoming track meet, her practices, and how she felt about them.

Gayle and her family lived in a very nice tri-level home close to the country club where they were members. After Cynthia had gone to bed, Gayle and Steven sat up with a glass of red wine to talk about their day.

Gayle swirled the wine in her glass and tipped it to Steven for a refill, considering how to bring up the extra-credit project that had their daughter so excited. Gayle had her reasons for not disclosing everything about her family. She had given her husband the short and sweet version of her family history, so he truly knew very little about them.

Gayle explained the project to her husband. "Do you have any information about your family?" she asked. "There's not much to go on with my own."

"Let me dig around. I know I have something about them," he said.

She couldn't reveal her family history. She had hidden the family secrets well, convinced they were buried deep enough never to be found. She had stashed family papers in the garage, ensuring neither her daughter nor husband would have access to them if either got too nosy.

As they got ready for bed upstairs, Gayle turned to Steven. "I need to finish something quickly before I forget about it," she said. "I'll be right back." She went downstairs to the garage entrance and scanned the room. Steven fancied himself a sportsman and had several shotguns, as well as containers of 20-gauge shells.

She headed toward the small gray cosmetics case, which blended in among the ammo cases. Cynthia knew better than to go near her dad's guns and ammo, so it was a good place to hide essential documents.

She opened the lid to find the old scarves and diaries she'd put there. Underneath that, protected in a zippered pouch, were all the details of her family's journey to America, settling in Jamestown, Virginia, in the early 1800s. The papers contained the details of her great-great-grandfather and great-great-grandmother making headlines for allegedly being part of a coven of witches and warlocks nearby.

The headline read: WITCHES IN JAMES CITY COUNTY ARRESTED!!!

The article stated that Gilda and Robert McKenney had settled in Warwick County in 1836, after arriving from the Emerald Isle of Ireland. The family had traveled between Scotland and Ireland for several years. The witchcraft practiced was not significant, but it resulted in being shipped to America. In the early 1800s, belief in fairies and curses was common. So, when Gilda and Robert arrived in Virginia, it was back to the usual for them; it was what they knew.

Gayle, however, dreaded the idea of this secret emerging, and so tried her best to keep it from her daughter and husband, as something like this would cast suspicion on the family and possibly ruin her husband's career. *Let sleeping dogs lie*, she thought as she put the papers away again.

Cynthia was struggling to gather information about her ancestors. She could find a bit on her dad's side of the family, and he assured her he had more information and would look for it. Her dad, his dad, and her great-grandpa were all attorneys, making it seem like a family tradition.

She traced her paternal great-grandfather as far back as the county and state genealogy records showed. She learned that her mom's great-great-grandparents had come to America from England via Ireland, and that they had lived in James City County. But where? And what did they do? Was the house still there? She didn't drive yet, but she had a bike. *Maybe I'll visit the courthouse tomorrow after school to look up the county property records. Maybe the house or farm they had is still there*, she thought. *This project gets more interesting each time I work on it.*

The season had begun transitioning into fall, and the leaves had started to turn. It was October but the temperatures were in the mid-70s, perfect weather for a bike ride. After school, Cynthia went to the courthouse and checked the property records then biked home. Now she had an address, which excited her. Was the house still standing?

After school the next day, she rode to where she thought the house might have been. At one point she stopped, checking her phone. The map on her phone indicated she was in the correct spot. To her right was an ancient, abandoned filling station. The sign was long since gone, probably hanging in someone's garage as decoration. Cynthia parked her bike, phone in hand. Slowly walking around the old station, she spotted an old barn out back.

"Cynthia!"

That's weird, she thought, not seeing anyone. *Maybe I imagined it.*

"Cynthia!"

She was scared. The sun had already begun to set, and the threat of rain hung heavy. The wind rustled through the branches of the trees and leaves fluttered down, at first softly, but as the wind grew stronger, they began swirling through the air. She trembled with fear, an icy chill going down her spine. She clutched her phone, wondering who to call.

"Cynthia… Cynthia."

She ran and tripped over a break in the old cement by the garage, stumbling to the ground and twisting as she fell.

"Ouch," she said, sitting up and rubbing her leg. She looked down at her phone, still open to the map. She was at the address where her ancestors had lived. Fortunately, she wasn't hurt, just embarrassed to have fallen. She looked around at the old property, noting the garbage and broken glass. *Glad I didn't fall on that.*

She stood and began exploring. At the edge of the concrete, she found an oddly shaped rock. *This is cool*, she thought. It was about two feet across, a perfect square, and slightly pink. When she reached down to touch the rock, it wiggled loose. *There's something under here.* She shoved the rock, hard, and it bounced away, revealing a book. A very, very old book.

Another chill ran down her spine as she examined the weird markings on the book.

"Cynthia…"

When she looked up, an elderly woman stood glaring at her.

Screaming as loud as she could, she grabbed her bike then turned back and reached for the book. She wasn't sure why but she knew she should take the book with her. Terrified, she raced down the bumpy road, back to neighborhoods and houses and people out walking.

When she got home, she ran inside, crying. *What was I thinking? Who was that woman?* Her mother came out. "What happened?" Gayle asked.

"I… I… there was a woman… a ghost…" Cynthia

could barely speak. Gayle rushed to her, directing her to sit on the sofa.

"It will be okay," Gayle said.

"No it won't," Cynthia answered tearfully. "There was a ghost and a book and a rock and I took the thing and that lady was coming to get me… What if she finds me here?"

After all her crying, Cynthia finally fell asleep, clutching the book she had been so upset about. Gayle reached over and gently removed the tome from her daughter's grip.

Interesting, she thought. Inside were stories about a voyage to America. After a rough voyage, the author says they struggled to survive, facing a lack of food on the ship and severe storms at sea. Upon landing in the Jamestown area, their challenges continued. It was a book of hardship, having babies, farming the land, and watching babies die from disease. The small farm they had was located just outside Warwick County, Virginia, and it sounded like there was not enough medical care for the growing population.

This is us, she thought. *Oh God, now what?*

She couldn't let her family find out about her ancestors. And she definitely couldn't let them know that those practices did not end back then but were still alive today.

I need to call her teacher, she thought. Gayle had known Samantha for some time, and they shared a common interest. They had learned the old religion from their families, discussed it, but mostly they met with others in the community who also practiced the old ways. It had to be kept secret, as outsiders could harm their families, and they had all gotten along so well in this area of Virginia without anyone knowing. Now Gayle was on high alert.

Sam answered the phone, and Gayle whispered, so as not to wake Cynthia, about the apparition speaking to Cynthia, and that none of this would have happened if it weren't for her giving this ridiculous project for school. "Oh no," Sam answered. "This cannot get out. My husband, your husband, the kids… this could ruin us all." Not only was Cynthia in danger of finding out too much, but so was the community at large, which could prove perilous to not only her husband but also to Gayle's husband and his potential run for the Senate.

Sam invited Gayle to join her for lunch the next day to discuss their next course of action.

On Saturday, Gayle pulled up in a Volvo wagon. Sam greeted her at the door and invited her in.

The home was a peaceful Cape Cod overlooking the river, and flower beds were everywhere; some plants were blooming, while others bid summer goodbye.

Gayle was a natural blonde with light blue eyes and a soft tan, making her eyes and hair stand out even more.

However, Sam could see the worry on her face.

Both ladies sat on the sofa. Gayle looked over the book and, toward the back, read about the curses commonly used back then. Sam smiled at her. "We've come a long way since then, haven't we?" Sam said.

Gayle smiled back and nodded. "We certainly have".

They decided not to allow Cynthia to read the book or use the information on her maternal ancestors. "It will ruin our families and our friendships," Gayle said. "We have never hurt anyone. We need to lay low for a while, so as not to arouse suspicion."

But the question remained of what to do with the book, since Cynthia was aware of its existence.

Gayle thought for a minute, and a slow smile came across her lips. "We change it," she said.

Sam considered this and agreed. "We can remove the old words and create new ones in their place. With some simple conjuring and a few friends to strengthen our endeavor, it can be done."

Gayle started calling some of their circle and received excited responses from them. They had not done this before; it would be a fun meeting. They planned it for the next day, a Sunday, at Gayle's home. Her husband would be out playing golf, and Cynthia already had plans with friends to go see a movie. Sam's husband would be preparing for his work on Monday.

The next day, they had the required number of seven, as

Sam's daughter, Lizzie, was also invited. She was ecstatic over being a part of this. Without Sam's knowledge, Lizzie had been researching the different realms of witchcraft and was entranced by it. Now she got to be a part of it and had told her mom Saturday evening what she had been up to. Sam was thrilled that her daughter was so interested, and Lizzie vowed to keep it secret. Sam had learned and embraced it from her mother, and it had been passed down through the family line.

The people started showing up at two pm. The sky was darkening, while low thunder could be heard off in the distance. Gayle worried her husband would need to abandon his golf game and arrive home earlier than expected. She was happy to see Lizzie and the others getting along so well; she always had fun introducing someone new to their craft. She hoped someday to teach Cynthia, if she ever fully recovered from meeting a ghost.

But she needed to cut the introductions short due to the weather. She called for everyone to form a circle, and they lowered the lights. They typically did not engage in that activity during spell teaching but did so on this occasion for Lizzie.

The circle was formed, and the book laid out. The words needed to be rewritten in the same ink and penmanship as the original. In the distance, the thunder became more ominous.

Gayle was interrupted by a phone call from her

husband, Steven, who was out on the golf course. She took the call, as they had not yet begun the spell.

"Hi, honey," Gayle answered with a smile on her face. "Are you getting rained out?" Steven replied yes, but several of them were heading to the nineteenth hole to talk about his future, and if anything, he might be a bit late. Relieved, Gayle said, "Oh, that is fantastic news. I have some friends over for an impromptu luncheon, but I think with the weather they may leave in half an hour or so."

She hung up and turned back to the circle.

"I think I found the perfect spell," Lizzie said with excitement. "Can you check it and tell me what you think?" James, a local orthodontist, was the oldest member of the coven and a practicing witch for over thirty years. He smiled and looked at Sam. "Your daughter has a real knack for this. I think it will be perfect. Other opinions, please." And several others voiced their thoughts.

The conjuring began with a prayer for safety, followed by the magical words as James placed his hands about an inch over the history book. The enchantment took about five minutes, and then, as all eyes were fixed on the book, a ghostly apparition appeared and cried to them, "No, you cannot do this. You cannot erase the truth… you will pay…"

Steven got into his car to leave the golf course, feeling that this was going to be a horrific storm. *I'd better get home before it gets really bad out here,* he thought. As he started to drive, the rain beat down, as though the sky had unleashed a monsoon. He slowed to a crawl to stay focused on the road ahead. Finally, he couldn't go any farther because the visibility was so bad. He came to a stop under an overpass. As he patiently waited for the rain to slow. a figure emerged. He thought someone was stranded and got out of his car to see if he could help. "Steven," an eerie voice called.

Wait… what the heck is that? It's not a person, he thought. He began walking backwards, wanting to get into his car but not wanting to take his eyes off that thing. "What do you want with me?" he cried. The Spirit laughed. As he watched, others joined, and he was sure he was losing his mind. Spirits began to swirl around him, making him dizzy. *Is this a Halloween joke?* he thought. Trembling with fear, he screamed as a hurricane-force wind slammed him into the wall of the underpass, killing him instantly.

At Gayle's house, thunder clapped and lightning flashed. The coven watched in horror as people emerged from the pages in ghostly form. The witches screamed, but they held strong. Sam and Lizzie held each other's hands, terrified, as they had never witnessed this before; it seemed that the words themselves were falling from the book, with new ones emerging. Suddenly, Gayle heard Steven's voice all around the room. "What have you done? Why have you killed me?" cried Steven as his spirit entered the room. His spirit hovered for a moment before entering the book, and words again filled the pages. James' daughter, who had passed away a couple of years ago, also appeared and entered the book. One by one, the coven's deceased family members appeared, only to be swallowed into the pages of the book, with cries and screams heard all around.

The spirit who had scared Cynthia loomed over them. "I told you that you would pay. I told you." Laughing, it disappeared.

The entire event took no longer than fifteen minutes, and then the storm ended. The room was clear. Gayle and the others opened the book to see that her family history had been rewritten, with no mention of witches or spells. The book was free from all of that. But the book was not the same; it now housed the deceased members of the coven's families, and those spirits would never rest.

About the Author

Ginger Adelstone is an artist working in pastels, charcoal, and acrylic paints. She is a retired photographer from the Myrtle Beach, South Carolina area and was a columnist for local newspapers there with a "how to" column, *Through The Viewfinder*.

Ginger has written several children's stories that are not yet published and is now focused on creating works of poetry.

The House

Sandy Hicks

The storm that had formed out at sea in a fury eased as it swept toward land. It washed ashore, wading through the marsh quietly. Once it reached the house and began tapping on the roof, the inhabitants woke, some of whom it would have been better to have left undisturbed. Seeping through the decaying ceiling, the rain slithered down the walls, bubbling up behind floral wallpaper, soaking the wooden floor, easing into its cracks. That is where it found things undesirable.

For decades, the house had stood on the banks of the York River, backed by the thriving marsh. As the seasons changed, it observed the migratory birds honking and singing in the fall as they paddled through the water, enjoying small fish and crabs. When the north wind howled down the York River, the house shivered and watched as whitecaps formed. Much to the house's delight, the marsh flowers returned each spring and bloomed in vibrant yellow and purple. Although rather humid, the house enjoyed the summer the most. The sun warmed the earth and soothed its foundation. Constructed from local pines and oak trees, the house stood proud, a shell with echoes of a time when it had emulated the happiness of its occupants.

It felt the presence of its new owner immediately when he walked into the house with soft leather shoes and wandered down the hall. Smelling of sandalwood and bay leaves, the human unnerved the house, tree scents emanating from his form. Dapper as any man of his time, dressed in a linen shirt that peered through a lilac silk waistcoat covered by a lovely wool coat that hung over his waist, where starched breeches fit snuggly below the knees of his silk stockings, the barber, as he was called, saw the house as worthy and moved in. He would use the front rooms of the house for work and the rest as living quarters. Having no wife, he hired a cook and a housekeeper.

Many who visited the barber came to be shaved and trimmed and returned to society as dapper as the barber, for he had skills with his sharp tools. In addition to being the barber, he was also visited for oral surgeries, mainly teeth extractions, as many had them rotting in their mouths. When the pain became unbearable, they would groan on the front porch until the barber called them inside and pushed them into his work chair. The house shuddered horribly as the screaming started. Although the barber stayed immaculate, blood and body fluids seeped down the chair legs and into the wooden floors. No amount of sawdust or cleaning could remove these scars from the floorboards.

As the barber's business thrived, he enjoyed more lavish foods. Pork barbecue was one of his favorites, made with a sweet sauce from imported sugar or maple syrup, followed by a confectionery such as lemon custard, candied plums, or an apple dumpling. His cook could bake a pie for every season—pumpkin in the fall, sweet potato and pecan in the winter, and all forms of berry pie in the spring and summer. While the barber's outward appearance remained impeccable, his teeth began to rot. The house knew he was upset by his deteriorating facial structure, as the barber startled and screamed whenever he saw himself in a mirror.

Around this time, the town began to buzz with rumors concerning the disappearances of young men. A few had vanished fishing on the shores of the York River and were presumed drowned. Some had been walking home through the dark woods after a day of hunting squirrels. Death was common in early American society and few saw the age of fifty, but to have a body totally disappear was a bit rarer, particularly in these numbers. Women stayed close to home. Others made sure to carry weapons to defend themselves if necessary. As men often do, there were many discussions in the barber's chair concerning this topic. The barber shifted uncomfortably and gasped in horror whenever it came up, such that the occupant of the chair grew silent for fear of being sliced severely.

Winter blasted in with snow and ice. Few visited the barber for trims, as it was warmer to keep what hair one could grow. The barber continued performing a few tooth extractions, but as with many aspects of colonial life in coastal Virginia, life slowed and people rested. Maybe it was the stress or the sugar and tooth loss, but the barber's cheeks had begun to cave inward. His lips sucked in and he began to appear as a withered sack that had emerged from the backwoods of western Virginia. The house grew unnerved, hearing the barber struggling unusually in the middle of the night, dragging gunnies up the stairs and across the floor, rearranging things. Then he would go down to his shop and cut and saw until the early morning hours. He sat exhausted as the cook arrived at dawn and scrambled him two eggs laid by her Buff Orpington chickens.

As spring arrived, the house began to notice an unpleasant smell of decay. Perhaps it was rot from moisture damage, but it didn't feel any soft spots. Maybe a rodent had gotten stuck in the walls over the long hard winter and died there, hidden to putrefy. There were unusually heavy burdens on the house's floorboards in the spare rooms upstairs in large cedar chests, but the house thought nothing of it. While the house contemplated its possible demise, the barber emerged into the warmth of the sun looking as dapper as the day he moved in, with a firm jaw and a wonderful set of dentures that radiated when he smiled. Business picked up again as men needed a shearing after the long winter. The smells of leather, sandalwood, and cloves filled the shop. The rest of the house, though, stank of something unpleasant. In the shop, many admired the barber's new teeth and kidded him that he should go into the denture-making business, but then there was the problem of lack of supply of healthy teeth.

While the barber thrived, the house began to decline. It sensed pain beyond the barber's usual work and could see the souls of death walking around upstairs, seeking a way out. Somehow they escaped the cedar chests as their physical forms rotted, drawing flies eager for a meal and a place to lay eggs. The spirits scratched at the windows and screamed in the night, such that even the barber, after installing a door at the threshold of the stairs, began to sleep in a room next to his shop.

By summer, the barber decided to move closer to town, leaving the house empty. Heavily, it held the burdens left inside. Trying to suppress the darkness when it finally fell asleep, the house lived quietly for years. The door to the upstairs threshold had fallen off from rusted hinges. The cedar shingles of the roof leaked, and termites had begun to chew the boards of the foundation. The house sagged as it lost its form in the same way the barber's face had. The rain fell, finding its way into hidden crevices. The house jolted when it felt them awaken and begin to move. Something evil was finding its way back, ready to take residence.

About the Author

A native Virginian, Sandy received her degree in education and taught children most of her career. During this time, she composed poems and short stories that explored the natural world in an effort to show the next generation the value of such things. She is currently working on a collection of poems about the seaside and an anthology of short stories that take place in the forests of the Chesapeake Bay watershed. In addition to writing, she paints in watercolors and acrylics and has works in several local galleries.

The Haunting

Susan Williamson

I smiled at the colorful displays of mums, pumpkins, and seasonal flags as we drove into our new neighborhood. It seemed we always moved on holidays: two Thanksgivings, two Fourths of July, an Easter, and now, Halloween. Being a Scorpio, born slightly after midnight on November first, I loved Halloween. I mean free candy, scary stories, and birthday cake to follow, what's not to love?

We were moving to a very old area, Williamsburg, Virginia, but actually into the most recently built home we had lived in for a long time. We bought it from the original owner who had purchased it from the builder in 1998.

Growing up, I lived in two homes my father built, then an 1860's farmhouse and a 1910 townhouse. When my husband and I married, we lived in his boyhood home for seven years before building a wonderful passive solar home in 1981. But we had moved on to manage a farm in North Carolina.

Our last home, built in the forties and remodeled in the eighties, had been the site of a drive-by shooting—the wife shot by a druggie, firing randomly out a truck window as he drove down the road. She was sitting by the picture window. We didn't know this history until the oil man can to fill our tank. He said it should have been disclosed when we bought the house, but we never felt her ghost, so it didn't matter.

At any rate, we had now downsized our ten acres to a duplex and were happily looking forward to living in Williamsburg. I couldn't wait to visit Colonial Williamsburg and take a ghost tour. The moving van arrived at eight, and we directed furniture movers upstairs and down, boxes to the kitchen, the basement, and garage. By noon the van was gone and the furniture was at least in the correct room, if not the final set up. Miracle of miracles, the cable man came and we had cable television for the first time ever, and semi-reliable internet. Hungry and exhausted, we headed for Cracker Barrel to get some lunch.

When we returned, the television was blasting. "Did you leave that on?" my husband asked.

"I don't think so. The cable man turned it on to be sure

everything was working, but I'm pretty sure we turned it off." I picked up the remote, noticing it felt a bit damp. "Must have spilled some water on this; maybe that made it come on."

We went back to unpacking. At five, he left in search of takeout and Halloween candy. Surely, we would have trick or treaters in this neighborhood.

I put sheets on the blow-up mattress in our bedroom, since our new mattress was lost somewhere between us and the warehouse. We collapsed in front of the television. That's when I heard the garage door. We looked in the garage and found the door open. I knew we had closed it. We looked at each other and pushed the button to close it again. Did someone else have the code? The owner had given us her remote. Perhaps a Halloween prank by someone who knew the code?

I turned off the television and walked outside to see orange lights on a few houses, glowing pumpkins in front of others, and a few masked trick-or-treaters wandering down the street.

We followed takeout Chinese with candy corn and took much needed showers. Then we curled up on the couch with a glass of wine to watch a scary movie. Apparently, it wasn't scary enough, because I fell asleep. I woke to the sound of my husband snoring. Gently waking him, we toddled off to bed.

I don't know how long I had been asleep when I heard

it. A loud bark, right beside my bed. I jumped and sat up. We had lost our beloved Labradoodle, Remi, at the age of fourteen, a few months before we moved. We decided not to get another dog for a while. It must have been a dream. But it was so real. The night had cooled, and I grabbed for the folded blanket at the foot of the bed. As I shook it out, something hit the floor. Curious, but not wanting to wake my husband, I got on all fours and crept around the bed. I felt something. *SQUEAK*. I jumped back and squealed. It was Remi's favorite toy, a squeaky green plastic disc. It must have been folded in the blanket when we moved.

My husband, who always claimed to be a light sleeper, continued to snore. I crept back into bed and tried to relax. I was almost in dreamland when I heard a thump coming from above me. Two bedrooms and a bath comprised the second story. Did something fall? We might have left a picture or something in a precarious place. Too wide awake to ignore the noise, I grabbed the flashlight I had left on the nightstand and pulled on my bathrobe.

I quietly climbed the carpeted stairs, using only the light of my flashlight. I walked into the first bedroom. There was no ceiling light and I had yet to plug in lamps, so I shined my torch around the room. All was as expected. The same in the bathroom. Taking a deep breath, I headed into the room which was directly above our bedroom. Although there were no sheets on the bed,

I had covered it with a quilt as I unpacked. The light caught an empty depression in the center of the bed. When we first got Remi, he would often sneak into the guest bedroom and jump onto the bed. If I heard him, I would follow him into the room, catch him in the act and scold him. But who or what had made this depression? Maybe I'd placed something on the bed earlier? I ran my hand over the depression and found a clump of white hair. I looked around the room and opened the closet to see if anything could have fallen.

There was nothing amiss. But as I turned around, the light caught a ghostly glimmer of white fur. "Remi?" I whispered.

I swear I heard a soft bark and felt a lick on my hand. I reached for warm fur but found nothing. Then something dropped to the floor. My light reflected on a garage door remote, complete with teeth marks. I wiped away tears and bent to pick it up.

About the Author

Susan Williamson is a freelance writer, editor, and novelist. She is the author of four mystery novels and a children's book. She is the editor of *Glimpses of a Public Ivy: Fifty Years at William & Mary*. She is also a regular contributor to *Next Door Neighbors* magazine in Williamsburg, Virginia, where she lives with her husband. Her work can also be seen in the 2024 Writers Guild of Virginia Spring Journal and several issues of Flying South, the literary anthology of Winston-Salem Writers.

When not writing, she can be found riding a horse, teaching riding lessons, gardening, reading, or hanging out with friends and family. For more information go to susanwilliamsonauthor.com.

Little Blue House
Narielle Living

A piercing cry woke Bridget in the middle of the night. Waking from a deep sleep, she tried to determine what time it was and why she was hearing a baby. Sure enough, it came again. Bridget began struggling to get out of bed, determined to reach her daughter. "She must be hungry," Bridget thought, but that couldn't be right, because her daughter was not a baby. How old was her daughter?

Thoughts jumbled, Bridget knew her daughter was older than a baby, but confusion clouded her thinking. There it was, another cry. This time, however, she was able to place the sound. "Cat." She closed her eyes and receded into her world of dreams, grateful she didn't have to take care of anything. Sometimes the house needed her, but not tonight.

The gray edges of the October morning began to lighten the room. Bridget lay in bed, mentally preparing herself for the day ahead. She should probably start making lists so she could remember what it was that needed to get done each day. There was a gentle push on her head, then the sound of purring. Bridget reached out to stroke the cat that had hopped up to greet her. "Were you the one who was making all that fuss last night?" she asked softly. The cat arched his back under her caress, and she felt the others join him on the bed. Laughing, she struggled to sit up. "I know, I know, my babies are hungry. Come on then, let's get you all fed."

Sitting up with a sigh, she felt around the bedside table for her glasses. It was difficult to see anything without her glasses, but then again it was difficult to do lots of things these days. Getting older was no easy task, and Bridget often found herself wistfully remembering her days of youth. Edging toward her late seventies, she tried to be matter of fact about the aging process. "Everybody's got to get old," she told herself. "I don't much like the alternative." But the reality was that she increasingly found it difficult to move through her days as she was frequently exhausted. "Thank goodness I still live in my own home," she often mused. "I've been here for almost fifty years and I'm not about to go live in one of those boxes for old people. Even if I do have to take special care of this place."

She shivered, trying not to think about all those years of care she'd put into this house on Crawford Road in Yorktown. Into covering up the thing that lived there. Into making sure it never escaped the boundaries of her property so it could not hurt anyone. She might not be able to move away, but that was fine. It was all for the greater good of the community.

"At least I've got my kitty friends to keep me company," she said aloud to the bevy of cats waiting for breakfast. "You really are the perfect friends. You listen, you don't talk back, and you love me just as much as I love you. Now, who wants some crunchies?"

Bridget moved through her day puttering around the house, trying to stay focused and organized. She liked to make piles of things so that she knew exactly where everything was and could reach it at any time. There were big piles and little piles, but everything she saved was important. Plus, the big piles served a purpose. The big piles were used to block exits. Exits that might allow things to escape.

As the late afternoon sun slanted through the blinds, Bridget decided to have lunch and rest. Surveying the living room from where she stood, she saw a house full of memories, a place where she had been happy with her husband and raised a beautiful daughter. It wasn't until her husband had died and her daughter moved away that the troubles began. The late-night rumbles and the smell of sulfur and the increasing awareness that something underneath her house was very wrong.

A sharp knocking at the front door brought her out of her reverie. With a sigh, she walked as quickly as she could to the back door. "It's got to be that nosy next-door neighbor, Mr. what's-his-name police officer." Exiting the back door, she took her time, using the side walkway to get to the front of the house, hoping Mr. what's-his-name would be gone.

No such luck. He stood on the front porch, dressed in his uniform and trying to catch a glimpse inside the house through the front windows. This was the reason Bridget kept the blinds closed, all because of nosy neighbors like this one.

"Good morning," she offered, struggling to remember his name. It was something odd, a word, Race or Run… Chase, that was it.

"Good morning, Bridget. How are you today?" His smile was polite enough, but anyone who would stand on a front porch and try to spy into someone else's house was not to be trusted. Bridget knew all about not trusting strangers.

"I'm fine. What can I do for you?"

"I just thought I'd check in before I went to work.

Your daughter called this morning, said she was having trouble reaching you and wanted to make sure you were okay."

Bridget sighed. Her daughter had bought Bridget a cell phone, a device she frequently left uncharged and forgotten in the kitchen drawer. Now she would have to drag it out and charge it up so she could call her daughter, just to reassure the girl that everything was just fine. Inevitably she would have to listen to her daughter's pleas to have phone service restored to the house, a concession she was simply not willing to make.

"As you can see, I'm right as rain," Bridget answered, hoping this would send the man on his way. "I'll call her tonight. I'm sorry she bothered you."

"It was no bother. She was concerned, and I think she has been for some time now. Can I come in to talk for a moment?"

Bridget shook her head. This man had no idea what he would face if he started poking around in her house. "I don't think so. I'm a little busy, but if you want to talk, I could come over to see you later." She stared at him, willing the man to leave.

Chase sighed. "Okay, Bridget. Just tell me, is there anything you need? Do you need any help with the house, or..." He hesitated, seeming to weigh his words carefully. "...or your cats?" A low growl sounded from inside the house. "It looks like you've got some new cats around here."

He needs to go so I can get inside and take care of this, Bridget thought. She knew that growl meant that it was working its way out of her enclosure. The thing in her house had nothing else to do and spent all its time escaping the binds she tried to create. So far she hadn't had complete success, but at least nothing had been able to leave the house. Yet. The cats helped, too.

"Those cats are my best friends in the world. I've been taking care of them for a while now, and we're doing just fine, thank you."

"Yes, ma'am, I understand that. How's everything in the house? Do you need any help with any repairs or updates? Any leaky faucets?"

Bridget drew herself up straight. "No, thank you very much. I really must be going now. You have a nice day."

She eyed her neighbor as he walked away. "Nosey Parker," she muttered before turning and walking to the back door. She paused at the entrance. This was *her* house, her sanctuary, the place where she could do her work. *This world has no idea,* she thought. *My little blue house is shelter to me and this entire town.*

Bridget was pleased with herself. She was not some old lady to be taken advantage of; she was fully aware of her rights and able to stand up for herself. She walked inside and said, "Just let them try to get me out of here."

Chase sat back in his chair, sighing in frustration and reaching for his phone. He knew what he had to do; he just hated to do it. He dialed the number he had saved in his contacts. "Hi, it's Chase," he said with a heavy heart. "I just want to let you know that you might want to think about coming up here for a visit. I'm not sure what's going to happen, but we're planning on going in there next week."

Chase closed his eyes as she spoke. Taking a deep breath, he said, "I have to tell you, I hate this, I really do. I know you don't believe me, but it's time to take some action here. Also, I'm kind of giving you a heads-up as a courtesy. Unfortunately, right now we have enough cause to just go right in. We're waiting out of respect for both of you. Can you come? Tomorrow afternoon?"

He nodded into the phone and disconnected. He really did hate this part of his job, but somebody had to do it. At least he could try to get Bridget some relocation assistance. After all, he wasn't without a heart, but he needed her out of that house.

On Tuesday, a crowd gathered in front of Bridget's house. A large number of official vehicles were parked out front, including police, social services, and the health department. Chase stood to the side, talking to an inspector from the health department. "I hate to disturb the woman, but I live in the house right next door," Chase told him. He paused for a moment, taking a breath. "Some mornings the stench coming from that house is unbelievable. I have a feeling there might be a couple of dead cats or something in there. We've got little kids; we can't be living next to a health hazard like this."

The inspector looked at him with sympathy. "You did the right thing, Chase. What're you supposed to do, live next to this forever? Okay, I think we're ready to go in now."

The police knocked on the front door and announced themselves. Opening the door, they tried to push their way in. "I think it's blocked," one of the officers shouted. Chase remembered Bridget using the back door last week. "Go around the back," he said to them. As the team went to the back, Chase turned to Bridget's daughter. "How are you holding up?" he asked her.

She nodded curtly. "Fine. Just fine."

In a matter of moments the team returned from the house. "Suit up!" one of the officers shouted. "We're going to need a hazmat team for this one!"

Bridget's daughter turned to Chase and asked, "What does he mean by needing a hazmat team?"

Chase hesitated before answering. "It means that the

conditions are so bad in the house that special precautions need to be taken in order to avoid possible contamination. I'm sorry, but it's got to be a mess in there."

The daughter looked upset. "I just can't imagine it would be all that bad in there. My poor Mom. She doesn't deserve all this."

Chase stood in silence and watched as the health department team donned white suits and went back into the house. The team was in and out of the house multiple times, conferring with each other and carrying full garbage bags to waiting vans. Approaching the inspector he had spoken with earlier, Chase asked, "Is the homeowner in there? Has anybody spoken to her?"

The inspector nodded. "She's in there, alright. She refuses to come out. Says we'll all be in danger if we make her go. I've gotta tell you, it's real bad. Looks like she didn't have running water for almost ten years, and there's piles of garbage and stacks of buckets in there."

"Buckets?"

"Yeah, she was using buckets as a bathroom for all those years." He shook his head. "Buckets."

Chase felt his stomach heave. "What about the animals? Are they…" He knew the answer before the inspector told him.

"We found some cats. Couldn't get a good count of how many and couldn't get near them. They all lined up, blocking a doorway. Weird. Maybe they have rabies?

Animal control's coming to get them."

"How could this happen?" Chase asked. "Why didn't the water company report this to us?"

The inspector smiled grimly. "The water company doesn't care if you have water or not. All they care about is getting their money."

At that moment a woman Chase recognized as a social worker was escorting Bridget out of the house. "This is my home! You can't do this, I know my rights. Don't touch my cats, they're my friends, they need me. I'm the only one who can take care of them… Don't move the piles! You don't want to move the piles! I can't save you if you let it out!"

The social worker led Bridget over to where her daughter stood. After talking for a few moments, Bridget's daughter put her arms around Bridget and hugged her. "It's going to be okay, Mom, I promise. I don't know why they're doing this to you, but we'll be okay."

"My home!" Bridget wailed. "They can't just go in there—they're going to get hurt."

Chase approached Bridget and her daughter. "Bridget," he said gently. "It's not safe in there. It's not good for your health, and your cats are not well. They need help. Don't you want your cats to be healthy?"

"My cats are fine," she spat. "Who do you think you are coming over here and telling me my cats are not well? Those are my friends, the only creatures that truly love me. They need me. Do you really think I would not take good care of them?"

"But Bridget, they're sick, and—"

"They're fine," Bridget insisted. "You're the one with the problem."

Chase didn't know what to say. Obviously Bridget was more disturbed than he had realized. *I hope she gets the help she needs*, he thought, walking away before he upset her any further.

Chase walked over to where the inspector and the social worker stood talking. "What happens now?" he asked.

"She has thirty days to get the house cleaned up and in compliance with our health codes," the inspector said. "If she can't do that, then we seize the property."

Chase sighed. "I mean, what happens to Bridget? Can we get her some counseling or something?"

The social worker hesitated. "She's going to stay with her daughter for now. Whether or not she gets any counseling is up to her."

Chase turned and watched as Bridget walked to the car with her daughter. "Don't worry, Ma, it will be okay. You're going to live with me now. Remember my house? It's blue, just like yours, and really comfortable; I think you'll like staying with me."

Chase walked closer, hoping to offer some words of condolence. He liked Bridget and hoped that she would get the help she so desperately needed. At least she had a daughter who seemed to be willing to care for her.

Bridget spotted him approaching and shook her head, almost in sadness. "You have no idea what you've done."

Chase sighed and ran his hand through his hair, watching as mother and daughter drove away.

"Excuse me, are you the neighbor who reported the situation?"

Chase turned and faced the social worker. "Yes." He offered his hand. "Sergeant Chase McPherson."

She shook his hand once. "Erin Washburn. I just have a few questions for my report."

She began to speak, but her words were drowned out by a loud rumbling. The ground shook and people scattered from the house, running in all directions. Smoke began pouring from the windows and screams filled the air. Chase winced in pain as the inhuman screams pierced his skull.

He saw a car come speeding toward them before it stopped in the middle of the road at an angle. Bridget and her daughter exited the car and hurried toward him. "You need to put the piles back," Bridget said, panting from the exertion. "It's going to escape. I tried to tell that man but he wouldn't listen."

Black, oily sludge began spraying from the front

window. Everyone took a step back except Bridget. "That's why there's so much stuff in there… to keep it trapped. That's why there's no running water, so it can't travel through the pipes. You've got to stop it."

When Chase looked at her with nothing but pity in his eyes, she knew they were doomed. A moment later, black sludge rained down upon them.

Bridget sipped her hot tea and ran her hand down the cat's back, stroking the silky fur. "Thank you," she said to her daughter. "I don't know what I would have done without you."

Her daughter had been the one to run into the house, to run to the danger and stop it. Her daughter had helped her find a way to plug the hole, the one with the staircase that went down. All the way down. By the time she'd gotten there, her daughter said the fires below were almost fully visible.

"I'm so sorry I wasn't here to help you sooner," she said to her mother.

Bridget shook her head. "I didn't want you to be stuck here. I wanted you to go live your life and be free of all this. But the truth is, I don't know what I would have done without you."

The explosion, the sludge, and the contaminants all combined to create a toxic situation that sent many of the emergency workers present that day to the hospital. By some miracle, Bridget and her daughter had not been affected. Bridget hoped the workers would not have a clear memory of what had happened. In the meantime, she and her daughter were busy planning a new solution so the little blue house would remain the fortress it was meant to be.

"We can do it differently," her daughter said. "We'll rig up an alternative water source, and I have a friend who is an engineer who can help us frame better structures to hold everything back. We learned from this, and we can do it better."

Bridget nodded. "You're right, we do have to find a new way to contain everything. After all, we can't have the gates of hell open so any old demon can come crawling out. I saw it as my job as a healer to keep our community safe, and I will continue to do so as long as I can."

Her daughter leaned forward. "You don't have to do this alone. But there is one good thing that came out of this."

Bridget smiled. Trust that her daughter would find something positive in almost having the entrance to eternal damnation opened for the world to see. "What's that?"

"I don't think you'll have any trick-or-treaters this year."

About the Author

Narielle Living is the president and founder of Blue Fortune Enterprises, a publishing company that believes that books have the power to change lives. She is also the managing editor for the Williamsburg, Virginia magazine *Next Door Neighbors* and has written hundreds of do-it-yourself articles for online magazines. She is the author of the mysteries *Signs of the South, Revenge of the Past, Christmas in Virginia, Madness in Brewster Square,* and *Birding in Brewster Square,* and she co-authored *Chesapeake Bay Karma—The Amulet.* In addition, her fiction appears in the Chesapeake Bay Writers' anthologies *Christmas on the Bay* and *Harboring Secrets.* She edits both fiction and nonfiction and loves helping other writers achieve their goals.

Narielle is currently working on her next books, which include a mystery in the Brewster Square series and a memoir about adoption.

Thank you for reading this collection of Halloween and Fall stories from the Chesapeake Bay Writers. We hope you enjoyed them.

For more information on the Chesapeake Bay Writers, visit www.chesapeakebaywriters.org

For more information on Blue Fortune Enterprises books and merchandise, visit blue-fortune.com

www.ingramcontent.com/pod-product-compliance
Lightning Source LLC
Chambersburg PA
CBHW010559310726
48969CB00009B/2496